THE PHOENIX

PROGRAM

Freedom is an illusion.

Raven Gray

The Phoenix Program

Copyright © 2020 by Raven Gray

Published by Blak Dog Group LLC

For information contact:
BlakDogGroup@gmail.com

Cover design by Labelschmiede.com

Phoenix artwork by J. M. Howell

ISBN-13: 978-1-7348340-2-4
ISBN-10: 1-7348340-2-1

First Edition: November 2020

10 9 8 7 6 5 4 3 2

CHAPTER 1

Beginnings

The cells were cold despite the number of children huddled in the damp rooms, but none of them seemed to notice anymore. After the day's training and tests, they were too tired to be concerned about it. The lead scientist Dr. Ulrik Jamison had been in a particularly foul mood that day and was even less considerate with the children than usual.

Dr. Ulrik Jamison was a brilliant but rude man who worked on the less-than-legal side of government research. He had a pronounced German accent and a brash way of speaking that only served to further punctuate his unpleasant demeanor. Due to his results, the government often chose to turn a blind eye to him and his team of researchers. In 1993 Jamison approached the government with an idea for a program to develop the ultimate human assets.

A series of daycares and were opened around the country with staff members trained to evaluate the children who were kept in the facilities. While, to the children's parents, they appeared to function as ordinary daycares, each child underwent rigorous mental and physical evaluations. The goal of the assessments were to identify the children with the highest cognitive intelligence, emotional intelligence, and physical capabilities. From over three hundred facilities, only twenty children were selected for the program. All records of the children were erased and anyone who had memories of the children were silenced.

The program, code-named "Phoenix," subjected the twenty children, all under the age of six, to further testing. Children selected were "reborn" with the sole purpose of being advanced and trained to be the perfect spies able to blend into any situation and human weapons so intelligent that they could predict their opponents' moves before they were able to act on their own thoughts.

However, the human mind has its limits. The experiments were extreme and unethical. They were designed to push the children to their breaking point in order to determine the strongest among them. But as many say, "genius is next to insanity." As the children matured, many of them were deemed too damaged and unstable from excessive mental strain during their developmental years. Those who survived possessed some of the most powerful minds ever recorded but were conditioned to be compliant and lacked the morals and understanding of society that children would normally learn from interacting with their parents and the natural world. Along with this, many of the children showed signs of numerous mental disorders associated with those of higher intelligence and a lack of social interaction.

Despite these challenges, Dr. Jamison refused to give up on his experiments. He decided to continue his work with or without the government's assistance. Over the years, rumors of an organization training children that were physically and intellectually highly advanced were leaked, but Dr. Jamison continued to advance his research. When the rumors were first made public the government denied any knowledge of such an inhumane program and no proof was ever found.

Outside of training, conditioning, and experimentation, as they matured, the top children were well cared for to ensure that they were in the best physical condition. However, the children were like prisoners and treated as tools to be used for the job that they were assigned. Many of the experiments that were designed to increase neural activity and mental functioning left the subjects' brains damaged or caused severe trauma. They were trained from the time they were able to walk to be human weapons and forced to fight each other. Those who refused were given an incentive, whether that be pain or simply access to food and water. They were trained to be masters of mathematics, the sciences, language, and the skills required to function in any job they might be assigned to work in. They were trained to be masters of deception, manipulation, and how to blend into any environment. The perfect spies, capable of deceiving even their creators.

After the first five years, half of the subjects had been lost, and the government supervisors were beginning to doubt the scientists. While conditioned to be obedient, the remaining children, ages seven to twelve, were beginning to understand their situation and becoming harder to control. During their first test run, the scientists quickly realized their experiments did not fully understand how much of the world functioned outside of the controlled simulations from training. Years of isolation during their formative years had left them with no life experience. And, when it was time to test them in the field, many of the children who had survived were deemed too unstable. However, a few of the children displayed significant natural talent in many of the criteria from training. These children were able to adequately deceive all involved in the test and were able to effectively complete their missions.

The four children that displayed the desired characteristics were selected to be used as a team in real missions. These children showed a willingness to do whatever it took to reach their objective. They were able to take down anyone who got in their way, hack into a database to retrieve information, and blend in to make it in and out without being detected.

Upon entrance into the program, after erasing their previous lives, each child was given a new name and two aliases created to be used on future assignments.

The four children selected were Corbet Chill, Matrix Cross, Blade Dangerson, and Ivy Blair.

CHAPTER 2

Alpha, Beta, Gathered, Divided

The four members of the Phoenix team were preparing to leave for their next assignment. The Alpha team consisted of Matrix Cross, code name Black Phoenix and Blade Dangerson, the Red Phoenix. Beta team was made up of Corbet Chill, code name White Phoenix and Ivy Blair, the Orange Phoenix. As per usual, Ivy was arguing that she should be on the Alpha team in place of Matrix. The two had been rivals since the beginning of the program. Ivy was always second to Matrix and the rivalry continued after their selection for the Phoenix team. The competitive nature of the two only served to fuel the rivalry, forcing their superior to keep them separated on missions. Matrix had the natural talent, genius, physical agility, and the ability to rapidly acquire new skills. Ivy was a gifted hacker and a ruthless fighter. Her willingness to push the limits often gave her an advantage.

For missions, each team member was assigned a task that best fit their abilities.

Corbet Chill, White Phoenix, age 14, member of Beta team, a tech specialist often in charge of getting the team in and out of tight security unnoticed. Skills include explosives, hacking, and advanced knowledge of chemistry and physics.

Matrix Cross, Black Phoenix, age 14, member of Alpha team, the most versatile of the team members, able to adapt to roles as needed in high-pressure situations, her primary role is the undercover agent. Cross is used when the team needs someone on the inside and is a master of deception. Skills include deception, linguistics, combat, weapons, problem-solving, lock picking and safe cracking, advanced knowledge of chemistry and physics, and covert operations.

Blade Dangerson, Red Phoenix, age 16, team leader and member of Alpha team. Dangerson is the most grounded of the team, his primary role is to keep the others in line and on target. Other skills include problem-solving, close-quarters combat, and sniper experience.

Ivy Blair, Orange Phoenix, age 15, member of Beta team, combat specialist and assassin. Blair is the most unstable of the group, her ruthless nature and lack of empathy for her victims makes her the best option when things go wrong. She is willing to do what is necessary to get the team out. Other skills include hacking, knowledge of weapons, and explosives.

While use of the children becomes easier as they age, the team of children draws unwanted attention in many environments. The assignments the children usually receive are stealth operations or where discretion is needed in populated areas. The organization within the government that oversees the Phoenix program and the lead scientist Dr. Jamison often argue over the use of the children. As Jamison's greatest accomplishment he believes the children should receive more important missions instead of meaningless reconnaissance missions or suicide missions. The argument was no different this time.

Dr. Jamison went to the head of the military officers who were overseeing the mission. As he burst through the doors of the man's office, the military man was already turning as though he had expected Jamison. "This is ludicrous!" Dr. Jamison exclaimed. "My team has proven themselves countless times in the field, I will not allow you to risk my work on a suicide mission to recover ordinary weapons that you lost," Jamison shouted.

Clearly unfazed by his outburst, the inhabitant of the office, General Haise, raised a hand to silence the scientist. "I am in charge of this operation Dr. Jamison," he began "and as such, I decide where teams are sent."

"If I didn't know any better, I would say that you are trying to get rid of my team," Dr. Jamison accused. The General's lack of response to the accusation only served to further enrage him.

After the staring match that ensued, the General sighed and decided to be honest with him. "Ulrik, the team is amazing. I have told you that many times, but some of the higher-ups are beginning to think it is too risky to use a team of children."

Jamison was outraged by this. He was not going to allow his life's work to be destroyed because some government officials deemed his team a risk. Had they not seen the footage of them in the field? They were amazing, unstoppable even!

Seeing the anger on the doctor's face, General Haise tried to explain. "Rumors of a child unit have already begun to spread. People are not happy about it, and the higher-ups are becoming nervous about what would happen if anyone found out."

Jamison thought about what the general had said before replying. "So, you are trying to get the most advanced team of special operatives ever created killed to cover yourself?" he finally realized.

"Doctor, we are talking about a team of children that were taken from their parents to be a part of a government experiment a decade ago, not to mention the sixteen children lost during the training process. Ten years ago, the people in charge were willing to look the other way, but things are changing. I hope you will realize before it is too late that we have to change with them." Uncomfortable and ready to end the conversation, the general finally said, "Look, we have worked together on this project for years, that is why I am giving you the courtesy of warning you. Now, the team is going on the mission they were assigned and that is final."

The angry scientist stomped out of the room, but the general feared that he had made a mistake in warning Dr. Jamison of what was coming. Unfortunately, he was right. Dr. Jamison had no intention of letting his greatest accomplishment be brushed under a rug to protect some government frauds from being exposed for their corruption. He was not a monster. He gave those worthless children a purpose. Now, they are part of something greater. Sometimes, you must make sacrifices in order to attain greatness. There is no way that he would let them take that from him, he just had to wait for his moment.

Back at the lab, the children were already prepared for their mission. He would let them go this time. He didn't doubt their abilities and knew they could complete the mission, but he wasn't going to allow his team to be controlled by the government any longer. He has plans for his team.

On the mission, the team focuses on their objective; retrieve the weapons. The airbase where the weapons are being stored is in a remote part of a forest, obscured from satellite view. Because of this, the team has to be airdropped a few miles from the base. Despite their internal quarrels, once on mission, they execute their orders with laser intense focus.

Once on the plane, the team begins going over how they will get in and out with the weapons. Blade pulled out a scroll and rolled it out to reveal a blueprint of the base. Pointing to one of the entrances, he looks at Matrix and says, "This is where Alpha team will be entering." "Beta team, you will be entering through this side door on the other side of the building," he says indicating the entrance on the blueprint. He then goes on to explain each member's job for the mission. Blade pointed to a room on the blueprint and identified it as the main control room. "Corbet, this room houses the computer used to control all functions of the base and, most importantly, the security system and cameras. I need you to get in and disable all security systems and cameras for quadrant three of the base," the team leader instructed. Corbet gave a sharp nod in response, and Blade turned to the next member of Beta team, "Ivy, your job is to make sure that Beta team makes it to this control room and to buy Corbet the time he needs to finish the job. Remember, the security is going to be tight on this one and the odds of you making it to that room unnoticed are less than twenty percent. Prepare for resistance." Finally, Blade addressed his fellow Alpha team member. "Matrix, after Corbet has disabled the alarms, we are going to be heading to this stairwell," he said, gesturing to the point on the map, "From this point on, the security will only increase. Optimally, Corbet will have been able to disable all automated systems and alarms, but the number of guards will also be an issue. Once inside, I need you to crack open the vault room where the weapons are stored."

The Phoenixes each nodded at their assignment before Blade continued, "Once inside the vault, Alpha team's objective is to recover any lost weapons that we can and destroy what we cannot. When your team's objective is complete, head back to the drop site and prepare for extraction. This is a high-risk mission. If anything goes wrong, completing the mission is first priority, understood?" A chorus of "yes, sir" was heard, and Blade nodded in approval.

As the group separated to complete any last-minute preparations, Blade approached Ivy. "Is the bomb I requested ready?" he asked her expectantly.

Ivy produced the C-4 intended for destroying the weapons that they would not be able to recover. "It's already programmed for ten minutes, that should give plenty of time to clear the blast radius."

"Raid-i-us," laughed Corbet as he walked by. "Get it, because it is us raiding them?" he asked still laughing. The others just sighed.

Oh, the hazards of working with a team of teenage geniuses. Blade turned back to Ivy as she continued to discuss the bomb. The last thing they discussed was the blast radius. All the rest of the team heard was that there will be no witnesses.

The team has been isolated since they entered the program and all records of their operations are closely guarded. If others were to find out about the Phoenix program, there would be major consequences for a lot of people involved, and those people do not want to be exposed for their less than ethical use of children. As such it is standard procedure for the children to leave no witnesses in foreign operations.

"We are approaching the drop site," the pilot called back.

The team quickly gathered their gear and prepared to jump. As the rear door opened, they jumped in quick succession, leaving only enough space to avoid a collision. They each landed with smooth, practiced ease on the dark ground below. "The base is two miles that way," Blade said pointing to the tree line behind them, and they began their trek into the woods.

When the team arrives at the base, it is still dark, and guards are patrolling the perimeter. They had gone over the plan in the plane, everyone knew what they had to do.

They split off in their pairs and made their way to the opposite sides of the building. The base was high security but due to its secluded location on foreign soil, the guards were not really expecting intruders. So, the two pairs quickly made it past the patrols and into the facility.

Once inside, Beta team headed to the control room as stealthily as possible. But halfway there, it became impossible to make it past security unnoticed. "Red Phoenix, this is White Phoenix," Ivy called into her radio, "The room is heavily guarded, we are going to draw a lot of attention. Be ready to move when I signal."

Beta team proceeded to take out the visible guards and advanced to the control room taking out anyone in their way. Ivy set a small charge to open the door. Once inside, Corbet quickly got to work on hacking the security system. Ivy stationed herself at the door and stood in position to take out any reinforcements. "Orange Phoenix, there are multiple levels of firewalls, this might be harder than we expected, "Corbet said.

"Umm... you might want to hurry then because there are a lot of unhappy guards headed this way," Ivy said seeing multiple guards coming from every direction. The first round of guards were heavily armed, but Ivy heartlessly took them down in quick succession. "I'm going to run out of ammunition before we finish if this continues," she called over her shoulder as she changed magazines and soldiers continued to flood the corridor.

"This security is off the charts for a small military base in the middle of nowhere. Grab a keyboard and help me get through these last two firewalls so we can get out of here," Corbet said struggling to break through the security measures.

Ivy continued to shoot and soon there were only a few

stragglers which she quickly took out before closing the door to help her teammate. "This is the first time you have needed help breaking into a system," Ivy teased. "Tell me what's going on," she said, becoming serious as she sat at the station next to the hacker.

With the two of them fighting the security system together, they were making quick progress, but just as they were almost through, two guards came bursting through the door. Ivy grabbed her weapon but instantly realized from the weight of the gun that she was out of ammunition and threw it to the ground. Looking at the situation from a normal standpoint, the fight was hardly fair, but these are not ordinary kids. As soon as the first guard stepped forward, Ivy pulled a knife from her belt and the guard fell to the ground. She then turned her attention to the remaining guard. Stepping over the body on the floor, she moved toward the stunned guard. Ivy smiled at the man as she thrust her knife forward again. The second guard tried to grab her arm, but in a flash, all he could do was stare into her eyes as he joined his comrade on the floor.

"Sometimes I think you enjoy your job a little too much," Corbet remarked after witnessing her complete lack of remorse.

Ivy flashed him a cruel smile, but just then the radio broke the tension in the room.

"White Phoenix, what is your status?" Blade asked.

Corbet tapped his earpiece to respond," Just one second and... I'm in. Security systems are down, you are clear to enter."

"Understood, good work Beta team, now get to the extraction site," Blade responded.

The team met little resistance on their way out, but the two still couldn't help but wonder why the security was so high in such a nonstrategic base.

Blade turned to Matrix, "You heard him, we have just been given the green light to move in."

As the two entered the base there were no guards or personnel in sight. "Most of the guards must have been sent to the control room," Matrix theorized.

Blade nodded his agreement and focused on watching for threats. Alpha team continued to carefully move through the corridors prepared for resistance but were confused when they still did not meet any security.

"Something is wrong, this feels like a trap," Blade said turning to Matrix.

"With the vault being in this quadrant, the odds of the base stationing zero guards or patrols around this section are..." Matrix began.

"We are both capable of calculating the odds of meeting a random patrol in each of the seventy-two corridors on the base," Blade said tersely, rolling his eyes at her.

Just as they reached the stairwell that would take them down to the level where the weapons were being stored, Matrix managed to piece together in her mind bits of conversations she had heard before their plane departed. "Blade! Wait!" she exclaimed as he reached for the handle to the door. "I have been thinking about some things I overheard before we left and things I have heard Dr. Jamison say. When you said that this feels like a trap, it gave me a base to put everything I have heard together. I have noticed that the doctor has been becoming increasingly unhappy with our assignments." Then with a little bit of hesitation, she told Blade the conclusion she had come to. "He believes that the government is trying to dispose of us," she said.

Blade scrutinized her for a moment before he said, "Dr. Jamison would never allow that. He gave us everything and made us stronger, useful, we owe him our lives. We complete the objective."

At the familiar words, Matrix snapped into compliance, and she nodded as Blade opened the door.

As soon as the door opened, they were met with heavy gunfire. Alpha team drew their weapons and quickly cleared the stairwell. They moved down the stairwell together as a unit, something they had done hundreds of times in training. As they turned the corner and exited the stairwell, they were met with several more guards. The pair continued moving forward and firing until they were close enough to physically engage the men, then holstered their weapons. Working together, they downed the rest of the forces with smooth, fluid motions. Their fighting style had an elegance that belied their deadly nature and allowed them to quickly dispense of anyone who stood in their way.

When they reached the vault, Matrix pulled her equipment out of her bag and had the high-security vault open in seconds. Alpha team worked with surgical precision to complete their task. They carefully destroyed any sensitive technology and weapons that had been stolen, recovering only what they could easily carry. Just as they were making a final sweep and Blade was setting the bomb to destroy anything left behind, Matrix noticed a metal case in the corner. "Hey, look at this," she called to the other half of Alpha team.

They both walked over to the container, and Blade dropped to examine it. "It's locked, can you open it?" he asked, looking up to his partner.

Matrix pulled her equipment out again and examined

the mechanism. She instantly noticed that it was a biometric lock, much more sophisticated than anything else they had encountered on the base. "I believe we may have discovered the reason security was so high. I don't have the proper equipment to get past the scanner, but I may be able to get in another way. The box appears to be made of titanium, but the hinges are not. High carbon steel melts at around 2700 degrees Fahrenheit, but it becomes malleable at about 2500 depending on the carbon content. There was a maintenance room on the level above us. You should be able to find an oxyacetylene torch and a large hammer there," she said turning to Blade.

Without a word, Blade was off to secure the tools they needed.

When Blade returned, they got to work immediately. Time was not on their side. Matrix first positioned the case against the wall of the vault so it could not move when the hinges were struck, giving the large hammer Blade had secured maximum effect. Then Matrix began heating the first of the two hinges with the full force of the torch's brilliant, blue-white flame. The hinges were not very large and began to glow red quicker than expected. She watched carefully as the hinge turned from red to bright yellow indicating it was ready.

On Matrix's cue Blade took aim and struck the hinge with his full strength using a very long arc in his swing to maximize the hammer's velocity. One down, one to go.

The second hinge succumbed to the hammer's force as quickly as the first. The case was very hot, and the door was still secured by the locking mechanism. It was unwilling to surrender its contents easily. Expecting this, Blade had also commandeered a pry bar from the maintenance room. Enlisting the hammer again, along with the pry bar they soon exposed the case's hidden contents.

The two shared a look of surprise. "Secure it closed. We need to leave," Blade ordered.

At the extraction point, Beta team was becoming anxious waiting for the other half of the Phoenix team. Just as they were preparing to head back to the base, Alpha team emerged from the trees with a portion of the weapons and an extra case.

"We heard the bomb detonate but you weren't answering our attempts at contact before that. Ivy was ready to leave without you," Corbet said jokingly. "What's in the case?" he asked curiously eyeing what was obviously not part of the weapons shipment.

"That bomb going off had to have attracted attention, we can talk on the plane," Blade replied ignoring the inquisition.

The team quickly filed into the helicopter that was waiting in the clearing and began the flight to the local airport where a plane was waiting that would take them back to the U.S. In the helicopter, Corbet asked about the contents of the case again.

Pulling the contents out of the case, Blade handed the unknown device to Corbet. "I was hoping you might know," he said to the tech expert, but the expression on the Beta team member's face clearly said he did not.

When they arrived back at the base Dr. Jamison was waiting as usual. He seemed to be in a particularly bad mood. Unknown to his team, he had another talk with his superiors who were now admitting that they were ready to simply dispose of the team, claiming that they were "too big of a risk." When Dr. Jamison tried to argue that they were even more powerful than what they had seen, the men in charge became more adamant, saying that he didn't have enough control over them and pointing out the possible consequences if he lost control. All of that just added up to Jamison becoming angrier with them and more determined to preserve his work.

The children approached Dr. Jamison slowly. As soon as they were within earshot, he was demanding a report. The team told him all the relevant information from the mission and then pulled out the device they recovered for him to examine. The doctor seemed very pleased, if a little bit surprised, and an evil-looking smile formed on his face. But when the children began to ask about the device, he excused them and had them taken away.

Unknown to the children, Dr. Jamison knew exactly what the device was. It seemed he had finally found some luck. In that case was a very special device that had been placed in storage many years ago. He had no idea how it had ended up in that crude base. It was a disgrace, but that no longer mattered. The device was from a project Jamison worked on in his early years, and it was time to resurrect that project.

CHAPTER 3

Testing Times

In the weeks that followed Dr. Jamison's talk with General Haise and the team's mission, Jamison began to push the children harder and increased the risk in his experiments. His anger toward the government led him to be vengeful. Unknown to the other scientists involved in the program, the doctor was developing plans of his own.

Back in the team's cells, the children were awakened to an alarm that had become familiar in their time at the lab. Despite the early hour, the team quickly readied themselves for inspection. As the doors to their rooms opened, they each were dragged out into the hall by a lab assistant to be prepared for the day's experiments. The harsh treatment is what the children are accustomed to and have come to expect. Despite the children's lethal abilities, they do not resist the treatment. Years of conditioning and experimentation, since they were toddlers, had been designed to also make them compliant.

As Dr. Jamison talked with the other scientists, they decided that they would like to focus beyond the children's natural abilities. "The brain is a powerful thing, I believe we have only scratched the surface of what these children are capable of," one of the lab techs says. "Corbet can read a 200 page book in seven minutes, then turnaround and recite it back to you, Matrix can learn any role and effectively become anyone, Blade can calculate probabilities in seconds, and Ivy has the ability to perfectly recreate and analyze anything she has seen.

They are truly incredible, but I don't know how far we should push them. Genius does have its limits," another tech argued.

"But, up until this point we have been focusing on developing their natural abilities and teaching them new information. I'm talking about tapping into aspects of the mind that have only begun to be theorized and explored," the first tech argued.

"They're still kids though; their brains are still developing. If I am correct about what you are talking about, the long-term effects could outweigh the possible gains. We can't risk losing any more children," the second tech countered.

"Take Matrix for example, the girl obviously is the most gifted of the four, she can do anything that the others can, and she is obviously holding back. If given the right push, imagine what we could accomplish with her," the first tech said.

"I'm just trying to say that we should be careful that we don't push them too far," the second tech said aggravatedly.

"Gentlemen, please," Dr. Jamison said raising a hand. "I have some very special experiments planned for the future," he said with a twisted hint of a smile while handing out files to all who were present. Just then, the men arrive with the children. "Good morning children," he greets them.

"Good morning Doctor," is the response delivered in unison.

"Please move to your stations," the doctor instructed them, "we will be performing some special experiments today that will be useful in the event of capture." As the children made their way to their stations where the equipment had been set up, one of the scientists came up to Dr. Jamison. "Is there a problem Mr. Thomas?" Dr. Jamison asked.

"Well sir," he began nervously "looking at this file, are we seriously going to be testing this with the children?" Mr. Thomas asked hesitantly.

"Yes" was the straightforward response he received. "Look, Mr. Thomas, I understand that you very recently transferred to this lab, but I started this program and I am the one in charge. Is that understood?" Dr. Jamison asked. Mr. Thomas nodded nervously and quickly made his way to his assigned station.

As Matrix made her way over to the workstation she had been assigned ten years ago, she mentally prepared herself for the tests to come. She sat down in the familiar, cold, metal examination chair. When one of the lab assistants came over to recline the chair and strap her down, she knew that this was not going to be one of the more pleasant tests.

After the lab assistant had strapped Matrix down, he walked back over to Dr. Jamison. "The subject is ready," he informed the doctor.

Dr. Jamison nodded and walked over to the girl but turned and decided to address everyone one last time before beginning. "I realize that some of you may be uncomfortable with today's tests," he said looking at Mr. Thomas, "but today we are just going a little deeper with experiments we have done many times in the past," he said finishing with a deceptively pleasant smile. "First we will be doing a pain tolerance experiment," he said turning to his assistant.

The assistant nodded and began attaching wires to the girl strapped to the chair.

Putting on a fake smile, Jamison turned to the girl lying like a statue in the chair. "Now Matrix," he began, "I know you can do this, so I expect you to do everything I say." With that being said, he turned to the device designed to deliver a controlled electric shock. It was not powerful enough to inflict permanent damage, but the machine was designed to stimulate the pain receptors in the subject. As Dr. Jamison prepared to deliver the first shock, several screams could be heard throughout the lab. He smiled, and another scream joined the chorus.

"Now children, we are just beginning. The more you scream, the harder this is going to be," Dr. Jamison announced. Putting down the controller, he turned to Matrix. "Remember what you have been taught. Focus on the pain and let it go. Don't try to suppress it, just change your perception of the sensation," he told her just before delivering another shock.

The girl tried to do as he said but as the electricity

surged through her body, another scream tore out of her throat. "Now, now Matrix, you aren't trying. You are only making this harder," he said before turning up the intensity and releasing another shock. This time the girl gasped but did not scream. "Very good," he praised her, "I knew we understood each other. Now, I expect that every time." Before the next shock, he looked at her, "prepare yourself, focus on the pain and dismiss it."

Matrix focused her mind and prepared for what she knew was coming. When the shock coursed through her body, she distanced herself, she felt the shock, but she did not "feel" it. "Very good," Dr. Jamison said again, "now we are getting somewhere." Repeating the process, Matrix prepared for the next shock. Just as before, she locked down her mind and controlled the pain, but as time went on, the shock didn't stop. By instinct alone, she began to fight against her restraints, but still, the pain continued. Somewhere through the pain, she could hear a voice in her mind telling her to relax and breathe through it. She tried to obey the voice, but her body fought against her and she succumbed to the darkness.

Sighing, Dr. Jamison told his assistant to take a break while he went to check the others' progress.

"What should I do with her?" the assistant asked pointing at Matrix, the slightest bit of sympathy seeping into his voice.

"Just leave her. We will resume when she wakes up," Dr. Jamison said dismissing any concern in the question.

Walking around to the other stations he was met with very similar scenes to the one he had just left. Corbet and Ivy were both unconscious in their chairs, while Blade lulled just below the surface of consciousness. As Jamison approached the first station where Blade was assigned, he checked the instruments to see how far the scientist had gotten. He noticed that the instruments indicated a shock intensity of about 75%, not as far as he pushes his subjects but not too bad either. Ivy's station yielded similar results, and he nodded moving on. But when he got to Corbet's station he found the shock intensity barely approaching the halfway mark. He turned scanning his staff and asked that the lead scientist of this station please come to his office.

The scientist from station four slowly scaled the stairs to the observation deck that encircled the lab from above. Dr. Jamison's office was in the corner just up the stairs and sitting above the testing lab. The door was open and the first thing the scientist noticed about the glass-walled office was not how neat the desk and bookshelves were or the plain grey scheme that seemed to cover everything in the building, it was the large window peering down over the lab so that Dr. Jamison could watch every move that his team made. Then, there were the monitors on his desk that let him watch in the rooms of each of the children at all times. It would be obvious that this man had some serious control issues even if he wasn't a psychologist.

Dr. Jamison was hardly surprised to see Mr. Thomas walk into his office. Gesturing to the chair on the other side of his desk, Dr. Jamison instructed him to have a seat.

"What is this about?" Mr. Thomas asked as he took his place in the indicated chair.

"Are we going to have a problem, Mr. Thomas?" Dr. Jamison shot back.

Looking a little confused, Mr. Thomas said, "I'm not sure I know what you mean. I have done everything you've asked." A mumbled, "Even despite my moral judgement," followed quietly under his breath.

Becoming frustrated, Dr. Jamison continued in a tight

voice, "I have been working with some of these children since they were four years old. I know them, and they can become lazy if they are not pushed."

"I was electrocuting a child for crying out loud! How is that not pushing them?" Mr. Thomas exclaimed, interrupting the doctor.

"Mr. Thomas," Dr. Jamison began again, "every other scientist down there were delivering shocks at 75% or higher. You were barely at 50%," Jamison sneered. "If you cannot do what is asked of you, I will have you removed from the project," Dr. Jamison said.

"But...," Mr. Thomas began to argue.

"And I do not tolerate questioning from my staff. Is that clear Mr. Thomas?" Jamison quickly interjected.

With a curt nod, Mr. Thomas turned and rushed out of the office, outraged at what he had been told. This is not what he expected when he was transferred to this project, and he intended to have a conversation with somebody.

Down below, the children were beginning to regain consciousness. The other scientists were beginning to prepare to continue the experiment when they saw Mr. Thomas storm down the stairs and out of the lab. Shortly after, Dr. Jamison followed, and the scientists hurried to finish preparing.

Dr. Jamison walked out in front of his staff and they all turned to face him, anxious to know what had happened. "Dr. Parkins, you will now be working with Corbet," Jamison said indicating for the middle-aged blonde standing off to the side to move, "Now everybody back to work." Everyone was a bit confused but did not dare to question him. They all turned to their subjects and Dr. Parkins quickly made his way to his new station. After only a short time, the lab was once again filled with screaming.

This continued on another three excruciating hours for the teens before Dr. Jamison decided to try another tactic to help the children focus. Walking back and forth down the aisle, he began to address the children. "Children, I am trying to help you, but you resist my guidance," he began in a condescending parental tone. "You must learn to control your minds, without that you are weak and vulnerable," he said taking on a harsh one. "But, I can see that you are tired, as am I. I have been trying to coach you through this experience but all you do is resist me, and I am losing my patience. All I do is devote my life to helping you, and this is how you repay me, with defiance?" he said as if he were a disappointed parent. "But to show you that I am merciful despite your behavior, I will offer you this only once. Up until this point, I have only been asking you to control yourselves for a short amount of time at a low input, but if you can only make it for say... a mere twenty minutes at only fifty percent, you may be finished for today. But, if you rebel against me and will not stay awake and stay silent, I have no issue continuing." "It is your choice," he added in a sickeningly sweet voice. He then began walking back to station one with Matrix and signaled everyone to begin.

The next twenty minutes were an excruciating fight between the burning agony and the beckoning of sweet oblivion. Matrix knew that despite the appeal of unconsciousness now, she would certainly regret it later. So, in spite of the fire that tore through her every nerve fiber, she managed to hold herself just above the line of unconsciousness. By the time the electricity finally stopped her body was almost numb with pain and the muscle spasms that rippled through her body were uncontrollable. In the distance, she almost heard the doctor tell her that she had done well, but without the pain to keep her alert, the darkness was closing in even faster and Matrix was soon lost to the world.

An unknown amount of time later she was pulled from her dream world by the heart-wrenching sound of another's screams. Still disoriented from unconsciousness, she tried to raise her hands to her head to help clear the fog but found that her hands were restrained. Being unable to move, she panicked. She didn't know where she was, and screaming was never a good sign. She needed to get out. A lifetime of training suddenly kicked in, and she slipped her hands from the restraints. A lab tech that had been monitoring her vitals turned at the sound and found himself held in a chokehold by the deadly teen. The lab tech instinctively fought back, which only served to tighten her grip as it increased the adrenaline flowing through Matrix. Fortunately for the lab tech, one of the doctors at the adjacent station injected the girl with a sedative. As the drug began to take effect, her grip loosened, and she was once again dragged into unconsciousness.

The second time Matrix awoke was much less eventful, and she was much more aware. Glancing at a clock on the wall, she saw that it had been six hours since the start of the first round of electric shock. Noticing that she was awake, the same lab tech carefully approached her again. He asked her a series of questions to determine her awareness and for a report on the success of the experiment. Once he was satisfied, the tech released the restraints and roughly dragged her to her feet. Another series of supposed muscle spasms sent her to her knees jerking the lab tech off balance. The young man stumbled to the side knocking the cart of equipment beside the exam table to the floor. The loud clatter of metal instruments on the cement floor brought the attention of everyone in the lab to the pair on the floor. By the time the others present came to assist him, the lab tech had already righted himself and was trying to decide what to do with the girl on the floor. With the help of one of the other lab techs that came over, he raised Matrix back onto the chair. Looking at the other stations, Matrix expected them to all be empty since she had been sedated for quite some time, but there was a still form lying at the third station that caught her eye. However, her attention was quickly pulled away by another needle's contents being forced into her bloodstream. A muscle relaxant she quickly surmised, and after a minute for the drug to take effect, she was once again whisked to her feet.

By this time the second girl in the had begun jerking again as the electric current was applied. As Matrix was half dragged and half carried past station three to the exit, she found herself involuntarily calling out for them to stop. Somewhat surprised, Dr. Jamison, who was now working with Ivy, turned to her. "You are going to damage her," Matrix said surprised herself at the boldness of her actions.

Smiling sweetly at her, Dr. Jamison walked over, "She hasn't performed well enough, this is for her own good," he said with faked sympathy.

Looking over at Ivy's head lulling on the table, Matrix knew that she was being pushed too far. She knew she had to do something, or they would break her. Ivy was not the most stable of the group to start with, but her skill had earned her a spot on the team.

Upon seeing the determination in her eyes Jamison sighed before continuing, "Sympathy is not one of the skills we train here, it was her choice to defy me. Now she must face the punishment. You were all given a choice."

Not sure what to do, but certain she had to do something, Matrix blurted out the first thing that came to mind. And suddenly, she found herself volunteering to take the punishment of her lifelong rival. This had to be a first.

Much to her surprise, Dr. Jamison had actually accepted her proposal. *Brilliant, look what you have gotten yourself into this time*, Matrix thought to herself as the last strap was fastened over her head.

Twenty minutes later, Matrix was unceremoniously dropped back in her room/cell. Her mind was more than ready to succumb to sleep, but the fire in her body would not allow for the easy escape. But exhaustion eventually won out and she fell into a restless sleep. Now Ivy was going to hate her even more for "showing off."

Several hours later her body jerks awake sending a wave of pain radiating through her abused nerves. Her eyes quickly scan the small, dark room but find nothing out of place to explain the forceful wakening. After taking a minute to slow her breathing, she ultimately decided it must have been a nightmare, and she laid back down. Her entire body was still buzzing, but if it were not for the pain, she believed she could find the sensation pleasant.

This time sleep does not come any easier as she replays the last day's events through her head. Things were not adding up. She was trained to analyze people and Dr. Jamison was clearly more on edge recently and short-tempered with the team. Not to mention, his recent experiments were becoming increasingly risky. He no longer seemed interested in steady progress, instead, he pushed the children to their limits in a way he hadn't since the start of the program. There were more of them then, and he needed to determine the strongest among them. Matrix understood that, but today was only one example of his recent tests that endangered the selected four.

Now that she had gotten started, Matrix knew she was not going back to sleep. Having made up her mind, she silently slipped from her cot and walked to the door of her room. Her movements were graceful and cat-like from years of training. Not a sound was made as she padded across the room with her bare feet. The door was locked as usual, but after a decade of living in confinement, all of the children had learned how to get past the sophisticated mechanism. So, with practiced ease, she made her way past the door and ran down the corridor.

Blade lie awake staring at the ceiling. When he left the lab all three of his team members were either screaming or unconscious. He didn't dare question Dr. Jamison; the man had made him everything that he is. But he was torn. He was taught to look out for his team. He was responsible for them on missions. How was he supposed to react to their screams? He was taught to kill those who threatened his team. "No!" he was not supposed to think like that! Dr. Jamison knows what he is doing, he tried to tell himself. That cycle had been repeating on loop all night when suddenly he was jerked from his thoughts by a soft knock at the door. He knew it was not a guard, they would never bother to knock, and neither would one of the scientists. That left only one option, one of the other children, and he always knew who it would be.

He opened his door and greeted the girl with a soft "hello" before pulling her inside. "It was risky to come here tonight. They are likely keeping a close eye on us..." Blade began when the door was closed.

"I know, but I had to see you," Matrix said cutting him off before he could finish. Her tone was firm, but the barely concealed emotion in her eyes gave her away as she visually scanned his body for evidence of damage the day's training had inflicted.

"You didn't let me finish," he said with a soft smile. She may want to appear unfazed, but she could never fully hide her emotions from him. They had worked together too long for that, and the concern was clear in her eyes. "I'm glad you came," he continued, "something has been feeling... a little... off recently," he hesitantly concluded, searching for the right words.

Matrix wanted to make some quip about how she thought he had been concerned about her, but even in the dim, warm light of his small room, she could see the concern in his green eyes that so closely mirrored her own. So, instead, she nodded. "I have noticed too, and with our recent missions..." she trailed off not sure how much she should say after the last time she tried to have this conversation. Much to her relief, he too nodded.

"I should have listened to you before, but I can see it now," he said taking her hands in his. Her hands were much smaller but no less calloused than his own. The years of intense training leaving them both hardened from use.

Matrix looked down at her hands, then raised her deep blue eyes to meet his, a sad smile on her face at the thought of what they both knew could never be. So, she released his hands, standing up to pace the small room. "There has to be something we can do," she said running her hands through her light brown hair.

But any response Blade might have come up with was quickly cut off at the sound of the door to their dormitory hall being slammed shut. They looked at each other briefly, and Blade threw himself on his cot and Matrix fluidly dropped and rolled underneath the same in one motion. Blade slowed his breathing to feign sleep, stubbornly clamping down on the panic rising in his stomach as the clicking of heels drew closer.

Surprise inspections always started on the boy's side of the hall with Blade's room being first. After that was Corbet's room a few meters down the hall. It was always safest for Matrix to come to Blade's room because her room was directly adjacent to his and thus, last when the scientists came back up the hall. The inspection was quick as usual. The two scientists that came briefly looked over the room, then proceeded to check the boy's vitals as was standard procedure after a strenuous test. Once they were satisfied, they exited the room, closing the door behind them. Matrix let out the breath she now realized she had been holding, rolled out from under the cot, and ran to the door. She briefly turned to give Blade one last sad smile before vanishing into the corridor.

CHAPTER 4

Out of the Shadows

The next few weeks consisted of mostly the same schedule. At the start of the week, the children would be taken in for Dr. Jamison's latest torturous training technique. They would spend three days training for the test, three days implementing what they learned, and then they would be allowed to recover the remaining day. But, at the start of the fifth week, no one came to take the children to the lab. There must be a mission was the general consensus.

Dr. Ulrik Jamison shifted the relatively small device in his hand. It had been a long time since he had worked with the team that constructed it. He was younger then, recruited fresh out of the finest university in Germany. But he still had the same ambition he assured himself fondly. Yes, the world would never forget his name. It was time for him to rise from the shadows and make his presence known.

"Assemble the children," Dr. Jamison ordered the tall but thin man that entered his office.

"Yes, sir," the young man replied with his shrill tone that always annoyed Jamison.

But it would not take much to press on his frayed nerves at this point, he thought to himself. The doctor let his head fall into his hands. He had been up most of the night making sure that everything was in place to execute his plan. It was almost time and he could not afford any mistakes. He knew his staff was loyal. He had handpicked each and every one of them, but the higher-ups were watching him closer than ever these days. It wouldn't take much to tip them off. With a tired sigh, he gathered his strength and stood to go and face his team, his greatest creations.

"Good morning, children," he said as he made his way to the four.

Each child was standing at full attention, "Good morning, Doctor" came the conditioned response.

"Today, you each have a very important mission," the doctor addressed them, a twisted smile playing out on his face. He then pulled out four black files and distributed them among the team. "These files contain all of the information you will need to complete your missions. Study them and be ready to leave in two hours," he instructed them.

With a chorus of "yes sirs," the group separated to prepare for their assignments.

After watching the team leave, one of the other

scientists approached Dr. Jamison. Of course, it would be him, "What is it Mr. Thomas?" the doctor asked not bothering to hide his annoyance.

"Are you sure it was a good idea to split them up, sir? They have never been used in a solo mission outside of training," he asked hesitantly.

"They are ready, the last few weeks have made sure of that," Jamison said in a low voice.

"You've been looking into the genetic advancements again, haven't you?" Mr. Thomas asked in disbelief.

"Are you questioning my judgment again? Because that can be very risky in this world, Mr. Thomas," the doctor subtlety threatened.

"Of course not, sir," he said with more force than necessary.

"Very good, make sure it stays that way." Dr. Jamison said eyeing him before returning to his office.

In their dorms, each of the children were memorizing their files. With Dr. Jamison's superiors ready to bury his project, he finally put together his plan to take down the government he had been forced to work for after leaving Germany. The files he passed out each contained information on a high-ranking, American government official and their location. Blade was assigned recovery of the Secretary of Defense, Matrix the Speaker of the House, Corbet the director of the CIA, and Ivy the chairman of the Senate Intelligence Committee.

The team met at the hanger door twenty minutes early to check their equipment before takeoff. As a group, they made their way over to a workbench and set out their equipment. Despite being assigned solo missions, the four hovered close to each other exchanging meaningful looks.

"Is no one going to address the fact that we are being ordered to abduct high-ranking members of the government we were sworn to serve?" Corbet burst out in a harsh whisper, breaking the heavy silence.

Despite his low tone, the outburst earned him a stern glare from Blade. Knowing that with the important mission, Dr. Jamison was likely to be monitoring them closely. Blade gave him a firm sideways headshake mumbling a generic, "You have your orders." Another heavy silence fell over the group. With one last fluid movement, Blade screws on a silencer and racks his gun with efficiency born of repetition. The familiar sound signals everyone else to pack up their equipment and head to the jet.

The tension didn't ease once they were in the air. Matrix fully agreed with Corbet. Everything about this contradicted their training. Maybe these men were corrupt, she trusted Dr. Jamison completely. *She had her orders and she would execute them*, she thought resolutely, slightly narrowing her eye with determination.

But..., then, as if he could read his teammate's minds, Blade turned to the group effectively cutting off her traitorous thoughts. "We will be approaching the first drop site in five minutes," he began. "I know some of you are apprehensive about your assignment," he said looking pointedly at Matrix and Corbet. "But it is my job to make sure everyone stays on task. I'm not going to be with you this time, but I expect both of you to complete the objective, understood?" he concluded.

Both nodded, but after a second Corbet looked up. "Hey, how do you know it's just the two of us?" he asked.

All heads turn to Ivy who gave a noncommittal shrug

before adding deadpan, "Orders are orders, I'm just surprised mine's not an execution."

It earned her three stares, there was an uncomfortable minute where no one seemed to know what to say. But it was Corbet who decided to break it with a chuckle and the whole group shrugged. It was a fair point, recovery of people wasn't really what any of them were known for, least of all Ivy.

The rest of the flight was fairly uneventful. Each member of the Phoenix team was dropped at their target's location and given coordinates for extraction. Soon it was just Matrix waiting to reach her drop sight. It was not that she was uncomfortable with her assignment, it wasn't up to her how her particular skills were used. Abducting a congressman was a job any of them could do in their sleep, but she was trained to read people. That was her specialty, and the energy before this mission was definitely off. Dr. Jamison was on edge recently, even more so than usual. Especially, anytime the military supervisor came by. It didn't take a genius to see that. The team was taught to serve their government and made to perform their best in front of them, but it had always been made clear to them that they answered to Dr. Jamison first, not those officials. It is not her job to question the mission she told herself, and with that final thought, she disembarked from the plane. She had a job to do.

Ivy's target was alone in his office. This was going to be too easy. Security was a joke. She really expected tighter security in the U.S. Senate office building. Not that it would have mattered, she thought gliding her knife across the last guard's throat. Just because the Senator is needed alive, doesn't mean everyone has to stay that way. Plus, he could have alerted the others she mused. She slid the bodies into a storage room, before closing it with a barely audible click. All that was left was the Senator. Smirking as she found the door to his office with his name prominently displayed in shining letters, Ivy didn't hesitate before entering. Definitely too easy.

Blade's target was currently in his mansion. The Secretary of Defense had an impressive security system for his home, but the gates were unmanned and the alarms easy enough to bypass. He efficiently loaded the now unconscious man into his own car, checked the evac coordinates, and pulled out of the driveway.

Corbet stood staring down the CIA headquarters. How did he always end up with the crappiest assignments? Well, he guessed it was his own fault for missing his window while the man was still on the road. Breaking into CIA headquarters would be fun, and to abduct their director no less... "And the others were commenting on how easy their assignments were," he grudgingly mumbled to himself. Sighing, he made his way up to the building. Maybe he could just start a fire, set the alarms off, and grab the guy in the chaos. He would figure something out he decided because this was what they were trained for. Even if hacking the security systems was his job and infiltration was more Matrix's area. No no no, focus, you've got this, Corbet chanted to himself, already regretting his first step.

Matrix's mark was leaving a meeting. The unsuspecting congressman did not even have guards as he made his way from the building to where his car was waiting. The driver barely gave her a fight, not expecting the young girl to pose a threat. Taking out the driver and leaving him in the alley almost felt like cheating. The team truly was trained for more... delicate... operations than the smash and grab abductions they had been assigned. Matrix almost thought she should be offended. The moment the congressman was seated in the back of the car she commandeered, she pulled out and headed for the evac site. The modifications she made to the seatbelt while she waited, kept the man safely seated and unable to do anything but complain during the ride. But, never say that a politician can't complain. Did the file say anything regarding whether the congressman had to be conscious when she arrived? Because she was starting to think that maybe Ivy's usual methods were not quite so excessive after all. Letting out a low, frustrated groan, she pulled the car off the side of the road. Matrix got out of the driver's seat and slammed the door behind her. Stomping her way around the back, she threw the door open and rough shoved a needle in the congressman's neck. "Eh, unconscious but alive," she shrugged looking at her work. The wait for evac was filled with the sweet sound of silence.

When Dr. Jamison arrived at his office that evening, there was a very angry general waiting inside. "General Haise, what can I do for you?" he asked in an innocent, cheerful tone.

"Ulrik, I demand to know what is going on here," Haise said slamming his fist on the desk as he stalked around the offending piece of furniture to stand face to face with the doctor.

"Now, Jerrold, is that any way to talk to a friend," he responded, his German accent coming through thicker than before.

"I'm not messing around, Ulrik. I just received a notice that there was an unauthorized departure from the hanger this morning and four government officials have now been reported missing. Tell me this wasn't you, Doctor," the General pleaded in a harsh tone with the man he once would have considered a friend.

"I'm afraid you left me no choice, General," the doctor sighed dropping his mask and also switching to the other man's formal title.

"I'm afraid you have gone too far this time, Jamison. You leave me no choice, I have to report this," General Haise said determinedly as he pulled out his phone.

But, before he could dial, there was a hand on his. "Jerrold, I can't let you do that," Dr. Jamison said in a deep voice, lowering the hand holding the phone.

"Ulrik, this is treason! I can't protect you from this!" General Haise exclaimed, turning away in frustration.

"I know Jerrold, I truly am sorry," Dr. Jamison said sincerely, dropping his chin.

"Look, I'll see what I can do, but these are serious charges," the General said with a hint of pity seeping into his words.

As he turned to face the doctor again, his eyes suddenly went wide with horror. Once they were face to face again, Dr. Ulrik Jamison thrust his scalpel deep into the general's chest. Dr. Jamison held his friend starring into his eyes as the horror slowly bled from them like the blood flowing from his wound. "I truly am sorry, my friend," he repeated lowering him to the floor, "but I cannot allow you to ruin all of my work."

The doctor rose from his kneeling position filled with determination, no time to weep over a lost cause. Grabbing a handkerchief from his jacket pocket, he wiped the blood from his hands and tossed it onto the body that lay at his feet. He then picked up the old-fashioned black landline phone from his desk. There was a soft click and a hello as the call was connected. "I need a cleanup team in my office," the doctor ordered coldly then dropped the phone to rest in its cradle. War is often bloody he mused, but it was a shame he had to dispose of the man. He had found him less repulsive than most Americans and would almost go as far as to say he was beginning to like the man.

With night falling, the children were returned to their rooms. Matrix stood pacing the floor, conflicted about what to do. Five paces turn, five paces turn, repeat. In frustration, she slammed her fists against the wall and let her head fall forward to rest against it. She had run the possibilities through her head countless times, there was no other explanation. Dr. Jamison is using them against their country.

On his way down the stairs from his office, Dr. Jamison was stopped by one of his loyal scientists.

"The device is working perfectly, sir," Dr. Parkins informed him.

"Very good, continue with the next subject," the doctor said, nodding his approval.

Parkins hesitated for a moment seeming to teeter back and forth on the edge of speaking.

"Was there something else you wished to discuss?" Jamison asked searching out his eyes.

"Well sir it's just that... well," he stammered.

"Yes, yes, go ahead and spit it out, Parkins," Jamison insisted.

"Well, sir... it's the children," he tried.

"Goodness man, pull yourself together. I haven't got all night, what about the children?" he insisted with irritation from trying to coax it out of the man.

"It's just that the children were trained to fight for this country without any consideration for anything else. We are contradicting their programming sir, I'm afraid it could have unforeseen complications, Sir," he quickly added at the end.

Questioning the doctor in any way was risky on the best of days and doing so while he was under this much stress was next to suicide. His words had been quick and a bit jumbled from nerves, and now he held his breath as he waited for Dr. Jamison to respond. Parkins could only hope that his concern would be well received. Much to his relief, Dr. Jamison began to chuckle, and he found himself self-consciously joining in.

Jamison scoffed, "I have worked with these children since they were toddlers. They have been conditioned to answer to me first. I have made certain of that. They won't question my orders."

Dr. Parkins smiled nervously, "Well then, sir, I have some work I need to complete. I'll see you tomorrow, good night sir."

As Dr. Parkins retreated, Jamison couldn't help but smile to himself. His children were loyal, they would never dare to defy him. They were far too familiar with the consequences of such treachery. Parkins meant well, but he had always been far too jumpy. Everything was going perfectly to plan.

CHAPTER 5

Question Not My Intentions

"I'm going to escape," **Matrix said with** determination, but as if she were trying out the words for the first time.

Blade just stared at her blinking. It had been three days since their solo missions and Matrix had seemed distant, but now this? "You have got to be joking," he laughed, "that's ridiculous." He would be lying if he said he had never had the thought, but she was just overreacting.

"Listen, I'm serious," she pleaded, "haven't you ever questioned anything we do here?"

Blade quickly stood and turned away from her. He let his head fall and in a low voice murmured, "you know that I have."

With a few quick strides, Matrix was standing right behind him. "We have to do something," she said seeking his eyes. Reaching out she turned his head to face her. She could see how conflicted he was as the storm clouds gathered in his eyes. But this wasn't easy for either of them and she needed to know that he was with her.

In Washington, things had been tense. Five high-ranking government officials going missing on the same day was hard to miss. No demands had been made yet, the press was everywhere demanding an explanation, and the public was becoming increasingly concerned. But what was he supposed to tell them? He was just as in the dark as everyone else. Suddenly, there was a rapid knock at the door. "Yes?" he called out.

"Mr. President," his chief of staff said briskly walking in, "this just arrived."

The president reached out to take the letter from his extended hand. "Do we know where this came from?" he asked.

"No sir," he replied, "it was checked for fingerprints, but nothing was found."

The president dropped his head, this was already becoming a long week and they still didn't know who they were dealing with. "I want every available person working on this, Jim. Send this out to every agency, I want to know where it came from."

"Yes sir, right away," his chief of staff nodded and briskly left to do what the president had ordered?

Twenty million for the safe return of each man. He

shook his head, that was a lot of money in the wrong hands.

Down in one of the labs on the base that housed the Phoenix team, the Secretary of Defense, a congressman, the CIA director, and a Senator were each strapped to their own metal chair. The walls were grey cement, the floor was dirty and stained, and the lights, dim and flickering, emitted a low buzz. The room was cool, like the chairs they sat on, but it had been hours or maybe days (who could remember?) since any of them cared. Three of the men were still clad in the suits they wore when they were abducted. However, the Secretary of Defense had been at home in his pajamas. The absurdity of the grown man in fluffy, blue pajamas polka-dotted with bunnies wearing slippers, starkly stood out against the scene that would be fitting of a horror film, the absurdity making the scene appear almost comical.

When Dr. Jamison strode into the room, the men did not even stir. Their eyes were glassy and backs rigid as they stared forward with unseeing eyes. Though their wrists were bloody from fighting their restraints, all evidence of resistance was now gone like they were different men now. *And in reality, they were*, Dr. Jamison mused. The device his team had recovered on their assignment last month had only required a few subtle adjustments. It had been nearly complete when the project was shut down just short of human trials. It was a shame really. It would have made conditioning his team so much easier. Perhaps more would have survived. "Ah well, that was in the past," he spoke aloud.

"It won't be too much longer now, gentlemen," he assured them. "With your government aware of my demands, it should only be a matter of time before your release. Are you ready for a new government superpower?"

"Yes sir," came the robotic reply from each of the men.

After Dr. Jamison's ransom note was delivered, he was presented with so many annoyingly trivial formalities. But, he needed the negotiations to seem genuine, for the return of the men to go unquestioned. He also wanted to deflect as much suspicion away from his plan as possible, and a ransom seemed the best way to do that. Eventually, he managed to reach a "compromise" with the negotiators. In reality, he had no interest in their money, but he couldn't let things appear too easy. The abductions had to be believable. The exchange was carefully planned. One of the hostages was set to be released, once the recovery team was certain he was unharmed the money would be transferred into the account provided on the ransom note. After the "captors" were satisfied the remaining hostages would be released. With the officials back in place, Jamison's real plan was ready to be executed. Not that he actually expected the government to allow him to get away with the money, he just needed the account number of a known enemy to take the fall. No problem for his star hacker.

Matrix was pacing her room again. There were so many conflicting thoughts in her mind and the tension on the base was only increasing. She couldn't go to Blade, there was no reason to bring her doubts onto him. But something big was going down. She could feel it, and she knew Blade could too, even if neither of them were willing to show it. But what was she supposed to do? This place was her life, she owed everything to Dr. Jamison. The choice was impossible, betray her team and betray her creator, how could she do that? Even if she were certain, going up against all of them would be suicide. And, what if she was wrong! There were too many variables. Work the problem, that's what she had been taught but what was the problem? Maybe she was the problem a voice in the back of her head suggested. Growing up on a secluded base in a government-funded lab had not warranted the option of exploring the reasons behind the orders given to her. So, why was she questioning them now? No! no way, her instincts had been trained to the point that they were not "just instincts" anymore. Anything she was perceiving was real. Something big is going down and she needed to pick a side quickly or she is going down with it.

"Steven, it's so good to have you back!" the President exclaimed, pulling the taller man into a friendly hug.

"It's good to be back, sir," the Secretary of Defense smiled embracing the gesture from his longtime friend. And, he was especially glad to have been provided a change of attire by the recovery team. He was never wearing pajamas given to him by his mother ever again. He shuttered at the thought of footage from his rescue with images of himself clad in fluffy, bunny pajamas cycling through the news reports.

The other man, however, misinterpreted the reaction and took a step back to look him in the eyes with a reassuring smile. The president then extended his hand and indicated for the man to have a seat on the couch. "Look, Steven, I know you just got back," the President began, "but we need to know everything you can tell us about the people who abducted you."

The Secretary of Defense sat down heavily with a sigh, "I'll tell you everything I know."

The Secretary of Defense spent the next three hours with the President and a team of investigators recounting everything that occurred since his capture. He began by telling about three men that forced their way into his home, one of which he believed to be Australian. He also gave him an approximate location of the base he was flown to in a remote part of Montana, as well as a detailed description of its internal layout. However, he had little to say about what occurred once he was in their base or the men that were there. Once he was there, he was thrown in a solitary cell and had next to no contact with his captors, he told his friend.

After he was satisfied, the President arranged for two of his personal guards to take his friend home. Once he was home and finally got rid of those obnoxious guards, the Secretary of Defense finally relaxed. It was late and the lights were off, but the full moon shone brightly through the full-length windows on the back off his mansion. He walked to a cabinet in the kitchen and pulled out a glass. As he reached to the faucet to fill it, he felt a full low laugh bubble out his throat from deep within him. The President was a fool and his "rescuers" idiots, soon they would all bow before the true Fuhrer, Ulrik Jamison. The man who opened his eyes.

Well, pacing was not going to get her anywhere Matrix decided. It wasn't fair to him, but right now she needed someone she trusted, and Blade was currently the only person who fell into that category. No time for indecision, she forced herself out of the room. The next few seconds were a blur. Memory took over and soon she found herself standing outside of Blade's door having knocked without a thought. This was a mistake; she had no real evidence that they shouldn't trust Jamison. Maybe she should just go back to her room. Too late, a rather tired looking Blade opened the door and she quickly stepped in from the exposed hallway.

It was late, probably about two am. The only safe time to meet was at night. Now that she was being forced into action, Matrix wasn't sure what to say.

Ultimately, it was Blade who spoke first. "So, are you escaping tonight?" he asked with a hint of a smile in spite of his tired features.

"I believe we both know it won't be that easy," she sighed, ignoring his lighthearted jab.

"What makes you think that we would have any right to?" he asked, tension flooding into his voice. "All of a sudden you are convinced that what we are doing here is wrong, but why? Dr. Jamison made us who we are, he has been like a father to us. What right do we have to question him?" Blade asked.

All Matrix could do was stare into the distance. He was right. She didn't have the answers to any of his questions. It was a feeling that she was not accustomed to. They were trained to be perfection, anything less was unacceptable, but right now she had no idea what to say. Blade was just staring at her now, clearly expecting something. "I don't know!" she finally burst out. After taking a moment to regain her composure, she continued, "I don't know, but we are not five anymore and Dr. Jamison is not our father." "I have been taught how to become a part of the world outside of these walls. We all have, but what makes us different than those people?" she asked.

"We are better than those people," Blade inserted, "Dr. Jamison made us better, we owe him our lives."

"Our lives? We live in boxes!" Matrix exclaimed, gesturing to the small, dull quarters that served as their home anytime they were not training. "There has to be a reason we are not allowed to ask where we came from or about our lives before training."

At the mention of them having a life before they were Phoenixes, Blade instantly stiffened. As a young child, any mention of the outside world in that context warranted extreme consequences. Conditioning at such a young age resulted in a subconscious fear of even thinking about the subject, and it was amazing to watch the change in his eyes from a look of challenging confidence to one of childlike fear. "Just stop!" Blade almost yelled and his eyes pleaded with her. "I am bound by oath to report any traitorous words," he said.

"But what makes it traitorous?" Matrix insisted. "Is it not a valid question? If there is truly nothing to hide, then why haven't we just been told? We both know that you are not going to report me, so why don't we find out?" Her words were spoken with all the confidence that her training had instilled, but inside, she was scared too. At the end of the day, they were both children.

Finally, something seemed to get through, and Blade relaxed slightly. "So, what do you propose we do?" he asked. And the sneaky smile he received in response made him regret he ever asked.

"We are going to get some answers."

And that is how the two teens ended up stealthily creeping around the base in the middle of the night. Their movements were precise, as they would be on any mission.

Once they had decided to go through with their plan, all doubts and second-guessing were gone. All that remained was the objective. The two decided to attempt finding records from when they first arrived in the Phoenix program, anything that would explain why they were chosen, where they came from, or their true purpose. The corridors were dark but familiar.

Their first stop was one of the laboratories. They chose one of the lesser-used labs to decrease the likelihood of detection. Night patrols were few and far between, the base was top secret and was not in a vulnerable location. The odds of infiltration by an enemy were very low, so security had become somewhat relaxed within the compound. Matrix and Blade made it into the lab with ease. It was dark in the room, but a bit of light shone through a small window on the back wall. After a quick visual scan, the room proved to in fact be empty and appeared to have not been used in some time.

Blade was the first up to one of the monitors and hit the power key. "It would have been nice to have Corbet along for this," he whispered, "but I believe I can get us into the system."

With a soft exhale, Matrix lightly shoved Blade out of the rolling chair, "Move over." After a few quick keystrokes, she turned to Blade with a satisfied smile, "We're in."

Blade appeared dumbstruck. They were all good, but none of them that good. "How?" he asked.

Matrix raised one eyebrow and gave him a slightly surprised look. "It's been over ten years. You've never seen one of the scientists put in his clearance code before?" she said with a mischievous smirk. At the look on Blade's face, she shook her head and turned back to the monitor. They were supposed to be geniuses after all. Observing details and remember important facts fell under that heading, even if they were not supposed to know the clearance codes.

Twenty minutes later, they were still searching for data on the Phoenix program. "There has to be something!" Blade exclaimed in frustration, "There are no records of us entering the program, training, mission reports, or anything." Blade put his hands on his head and paced in a small circle around the room. It was like they never even existed. He trudged his way back over to Matrix and put both palms on the desk with his head low. "You are sure there is not another security code or a hidden file?" he asked.

"No, we've already checked everything three times," Matrix said equally as frustrated. "Maybe we should just go back to our rooms before someone notices we left," she suggested. Neither of them wanted to do that, but she knew they were taking a big risk being there.

"But there is no way we could live on this base for over a decade without so much as a training schedule," Blade protested. He may have been against this in the beginning, but there was no way he was giving up now. Their mission was incomplete.

"I know, but what else can we do?" she asked.

"Wait, you said that something big is happening, right?" Blade asked suddenly standing up straight.

"Yes," Matrix replied hesitantly. She could sense a point was coming, and he had her full attention.

"Remember that mission to recover a shipment of weapons last month?" he continued. Matrix nodded beginning to piece together where he was going with this. "You thought that Dr. Jamison was angry with the government for trying to dispose of our team and with the recent missions..."

"Dr. Jamison is taking revenge on them for threatening

us," Matrix finished for him.

"And, he likely deleted our files so that the government couldn't get their hands on them," Blade added.

Smiling Matrix turned back to the keyboard, now that she knew what to look for, recovering the files should be easy.

"This is great," Blade said hopefully, "Dr. Jamison is just protecting us."

Their theory made sense, but something still did not feel right to Matrix. "Yeah, it is," she replied a bit monotone in comparison to Blade.

"What? You don't agree?" he asked confused by her tone. Matrix thought about the question for a second. Nothing she thought she knew seemed to be accurate anymore. "I don't know. I will be happy once we get some real answers from these files," she finally said.

The time while Blade waited for Matrix to recover the deleted data was tense. He wanted to believe that Dr. Jamison was trying to protect them, but for some reason, Matrix seemed determined to question his motives. He was like a father to them. They would be nothing without him. The phrase rang out in his mind, just as it always had. He had heard it many times as a child, they all had. It was the only truth he had ever known, and it was difficult for him to even consider questioning it. Soon, though, he was pulled out of his thoughts by a video file.

"Most of the data was corrupted," Matrix informed him. "But, I was able to salvage a few files before they were permanently destroyed," she said. But, despite the triumph of her words, there were dark undercurrents in her tone. Blade, however, was already absorbed in the video playing on the screen.

"The children are advancing well," the man in the video

said. The two teens could already tell who it was from the accented voice but waited anxiously as the man turned to address the camera. He had slightly more hair and he wore no glasses, but the man that turned around was unmistakably a younger version of Jamison. The video file was recorded not very long after the Phoenix program was initiated. The scene had all the appearances of a typical kindergarten classroom. In the room with him were twenty children, each sitting at a tiny desk with a test in front of them. Blade and Matrix knew the room well. They had spent much of their childhood inside those four grey walls. Outside of physical training, most of their time was spent training their mental gifts. The room had evolved with the children over the years, but one could argue that neither changed for the better. As they advanced, the tests became more difficult and advanced well beyond standard knowledge for children. The innocent appearing scene that played out on the screen was only the beginning for the twenty children removed from their lives.

"I remember this day," Matrix murmured, barely above a whisper. Perfect recall, it was not uncommon among the original twenty, but Matrix and Ivy were the only two remaining with the attribute. Blade knew this, and thus, didn't comment as he waited for the scene to unfold.

The man they now knew to be Dr. Jamison turned away from the camera again and strode over to the nearest desk. He then reached a hand under his lab coat and produced a metal rod. Taking the rod into his left hand and with a swift motion he cracked it against the desk. There was not a child or scientist in the room who didn't flinch, and many of the children were frightened to tears. As if nothing had happened, the doctor made his way to the first desk and began to collect the test. "Time is up," he announced with a calm but cynical note. Both of the teens watching the video flinched at the tone as he spoke to the children on the screen. Despite knowing it was a recording, that particular tone always was followed by an unpleasant stimulus. After Dr. Jamison collected the last test, he once again brought the metal down against a desk. When the children once again screamed, he told them that their response was unacceptable. "I want to help you," he said, "In this world, you must show no weakness. If we are to flinch at every sound, the enemy will always have the upper hand. I want to make you strong. Do not show your fear!" By the end of his speech, his words had gone from sickeningly sweet to a harsh rant. With the room still filled with soft sobs, Dr. Jamison turned to one of the other, rather shaken, scientists in the room. Dr. Jamison passed a judgmental glance over the man seeming to consider what he wanted to say. The other scientist, whose name neither of the two teens had heard, nervously avoided Dr. Jamison's eyes. However, much to the man's relief, he appeared uninterested in reprimanding him in front of the children. He instead gestured with an outstretched arm toward the children. "After they have regained control of themselves, they may be dismissed," he instructed the man.

At that point, the video shook briefly and went blank. Blade swallowed hard. It was much different watching that from the outside. He remembered the metal rod well. They had been conditioned not to react to the sound that came to signal the end of a test. For much of the video, his eyes had been drawn to a six-year-old boy on the back row. His hair was thick, raven black, and his bangs low on his forehead almost reached his green eyes. The boy cried just like most of the others and tears streamed down his lightly tanned cheeks. After watching the scene, Blade also remembered that day. "What was the label of the video file?" he asked

Matrix. His voice was low, and his body was numb, but he knew that this was not the time for emotion. He turned to Matrix whose eyes were still transfixed on the black screen. He recognized the look. All of the same memories he could read on her face had played through his mind only moments ago. "Matrix?" he tried again.

The sound of her name seemed to break her from the unpleasant reverie, and she shook her head slightly to clear the remaining thoughts. With a few quick keystrokes the file was closed and the name on the screen, "Experiment 04: Noise Reaction Training." "Experiment. It was all an experiment. Our entire lives have been an experiment," she whispered. Matrix's eyes were haunted by all of the memories from their past.

"What else did you recover?" Blade asked, grabbing the keyboard to turn it for both of his hands to use.

"Not much, most of the files have been corrupted. But, if you are right, Dr. Jamison would not have deleted all of his..." she fumbled slightly for the right word, "research on us without making a copy."

"Research," Blade repeated, "Could that really be all we are to him?"

"I don't know," Matrix sighed. This was their life. Surely not everything was an experiment.

Blade was angry or sad or confused. He didn't know what he was at this point, but he didn't have the convenience to ponder it any further.

"I hear voices," Matrix alerted him, and a beam of light flashed across the frosted window of the door. "We need to go!" she urged.

"But what about the other files?" Blade protested.

"Leave it. The doctor must have backups somewhere on site. He wouldn't destroy his work. We can look for them later, but right now we need to go!"

Before Blade had a chance to protest any further, Matrix had already taken the keyboard back and began covering any evidence that they had ever recovered the files. With that complete, they quickly slipped from the room and silently ran down the hall, careful to not alert the guards that had stopped to chat around the corner.

Once they had made their way back to their rooms, they gave each other one last look and closed their doors. A lot had changed that night and neither of them were certain what those changes would bring. This life was all they knew, but escaping did not sound quite as crazy as it had before.

CHAPTER 6

What's My Name?

It was late at night again. Things had been calm on the base the last few nights, and everything was beginning to feel too calm, like the calm before the storm. After piecing together Dr. Jamison's plan, Matrix and Blade had done their best to gather as much information about the Phoenix Program and where their records could be located as possible. On the third night, they decided they had done as much reconnaissance as possible and it was time to make a move.

"It's now or never, we need to do this," Matrix said.

"We are ready," Blade replied with a confident nod of his head.

They had determined where the base archives were but knowing that Dr. Jamison was a paranoid and suspicious man, the only logical place he would store his research would be locked away in his office. Breaking into his office undetected would be one of the biggest challenges they had ever faced. Especially knowing that if they got caught, shooting their way out was not likely to be an option. Most bases they infiltrated were designed to keep people out, but this base was also designed to keep people in. His office was above their main testing lab. The room was large and open. It closely resembled a factory where the work was performed below, but the boss could sit in his office above and watch over his workers through the glass observatory of his office.

The base was old, and the lab particularly showed its age at night. The lights that hung overhead gave off a cool, dim cone of light, each highlighting the chair at the station over which they loomed. They buzzed and flickered giving off the minimum light for the night shift. Dr. Jamison's office however stood in striking contrast. His pristine office was a relatively new addition to the base, and the man had spared no expense in designing it. The security system was of his own design. A palm scan and a twelve-digit passcode were required to open the door. Once inside, on the opposite wall, there was another hidden panel that required a scan of the other hand. It was designed so that if someone managed to break into the office, they would believe they had bypassed all of the security measures. If the other palm scan was not produced within thirty seconds, alarms would sound, and steel bars would lock down the room. Within the room, all of his filing cabinets had fingerprint scanners and his computers were heavily encrypted. In the far-right corner of the room there was a safe, slightly old fashioned, but immune to hacking. The outer shell was constructed of titanium and the pistons were heavily silenced. It was unlikely that anyone would make it that far. Even if they did, the safe would present even the most experienced thieves with a challenge.

The two quickly and quietly made their way to Dr. Jamison's office. They had gathered as much additional information about the room as possible and were confident they could complete their missions. Each had been briefed in his office on multiple occasions, but the security measures had not been active at the time. Blade was the only one that had actually seen Dr. Jamison perform the ritual required to access the room. Based on his hand positioning when he entered his code, Blade was fairly certain what the twelve digits were. But, Matrix had argued that it was too risky to try the code. They had no idea how the system would respond if the wrong code was entered. Guessing could end their mission before it truly began. So instead, when they reached the door, Blade motioned Matrix forward and turned to stand guard while she worked. They were both competent hackers, but with Matrix's advanced training in locks and safes, it was decided before they left that she would be the one to get them in.

Before moving up to the second level where Dr. Jamison's office was, they stopped to grab their mission gear. Even with the state-of-the-art equipment they had, hacking the hand scanner to make it believe the correct scan had been entered was challenging for the highly trained teen, but after a few minutes, Matrix was able to bypass the first security measure. Matrix then used a cable to connect her laptop to the keypad. Using Blade's guess for the access code as a starting point, the algorithm programmed into the laptop quickly determined that Blade did indeed have the correct access code. A fact he was unnaturally proud to have proven.

As soon as the door unlocked, they moved as quickly as possible to the hidden panel on the opposite wall. Bypassing the first scanner had taken several minutes. They had a much better starting point after working with the first scanner, but with the second needing the opposite hand, Matrix would need every second to finish.

Blade started to mentally time her progress so that he could alert her when time was about to run out. Just as he was beginning to believe they were about to run out of time, the scanner pad lit up green and Matrix looked up to him with a satisfied smirk.

"Twenty-seven seconds, I'm impressed," he said, "I wasn't sure you were going to make it."

Matrix rolled her eyes, "I work best under pressure."

"Well, we made it past the first test. Do you think you can get past that safe?" Blade asked gesturing to the vault in the corner.

Matrix walked over to the safe and kneeled before it, running an assessing gaze over the metal container. Placing her hand on the cool metal of the dial, she turned it experimentally. The well-oiled dial turned smoothly and silently, unwilling to give up any of its secrets so easily. Reaching into her bag, she felt around in the semi-dark for a moment before her hand found the correct tool. Her hand emerged with a tool Blade had seen her use several times. She then placed the small, black cube against the safe, near where the tumblers and drive pin would be located. On the side that was facing her, a glass screen covered the sensitive dial. Matrix had designed the device herself. It was similar to a highly sensitive seismograph. The magnetic bottom secured it to the safe to avoid the device being unnecessarily shaken while a needle on the front displayed all vibrations. In addition, a set of headphones could be plugged in to allow her to listen as one would with a stethoscope. It had proven quite useful on many missions, and she was very proud of the design. With the headphones in, Matrix got to work turning the dial. After a few turns around, she believed she had determined the first number. She made a mental note and continued in the opposite direction repeating the process until, with a satisfied smirk, she gave the handle a firm turn. The sound of the safe opening drew Blade's attention away from the doorway where he had positioned himself as a guard.

The pair gazed into the open safe with a conflicting mix of relief and apprehension. The large safe contained many files, hard drives, videotapes, and DVDs. Some of them looked as though they had not been touched in years, but in the front, a large stack seemed to have been recently added, while the surrounding files had been pushed away to clear space. Blade was the first that seemed to recover from the thought that they could finally have answers to all of their questions. His hand reached out to grab a small hard drive from the top and Matrix didn't miss the slight tremor in his hand as he did so. He then stiffly shouldered off his bag and removed his own laptop. Blade unnaturally fumbled with the cord and Matrix gently took it from him and connected the hard drive. She nudged him lightly in the shoulder. "Having second thoughts?" she picked in an attempt to lighten the mood. Blade made a weak attempt at a smile in response to her teasing tone, but the gesture did not reach his eyes.

The next twenty minutes were spent sifting through large amounts of data. The deeper they went, the more disturbing their findings became. Results from tests, mission, reports, team evaluations, everything was there. This was it; they were finally getting answers. Seeing all of their training results written down in lab reports was surreal, but they continued moving back in time.

"This is it, I found it!" Blade exclaimed in a harsh whisper. In the folder he opened, there were the profiles of twenty children.

"The names, they don't match the faces," Matrix instantly noticed as Blade rotated through. The impact of the new information felt like she had been punched in the stomach, and she was fighting to control her breath. "We spent years with these children and we never even knew their names," she whispered so quietly Blade barely even heard her.

A quick intake of breath had Matrix's eyes darting way from her reverie and up to Blade. His eyes were glued to the screen and his hands were slightly shaking again. It was as though he had seen a ghost. And the two words he spoke sent a wave of memories, long since buried, rushing through his mind. "Duran Creed." He momentarily had to fight the burning in his eyes. It felt as though he was being drawn back into a time he was forced to forget years ago.

They shared a look for a long moment before Matrix finally managed to ask, "What is my name?"

Blade's numb fingers flicked through a few more profiles before finally settling on a young girl with blue eyes and wavy brown hair. Beneath the image was a name that Blade read aloud, "Varian Ledger."

Unsure what to do next, they both sat in silence, each trying to process that they had a life before the program. Neither offered to comfort the other. They both knew that neither of them would want that right now. Matrix knew that they needed to get out of Jamison's office, but right now Blade, or now Duran she guessed, seemed miles away. His unblinking stare fixed on an undescriptive spot on the wall.

A part of herself that she was forced to purge years ago, urged her to ask if he was alright. She was not the comforting type, but she had been taught how to make someone comfortable. It had come in handy many times on assignment. However, knowing how betrayed she felt, Matrix did not believe it would be wise or safe to try to manipulate her teammate right now. Not that she knew what to say anyway, she mused. It's hard to save someone else's ship when the waters are threatening to overtake your own.

Matrix didn't know how long she had been sitting curled up in the corner of Jamison's office when alarms started sounding across the base. Both her and Blade were instantly on high alert, all of their inward turmoil shoved to the side. It was almost a relief, and Matrix had to fight to smother the inappropriate laugh that threatened to bubble over. Blade had not moved in what had to be an hour. She thought he might have been frozen into a statue by shock. At least this way she didn't have to fight for a way to pierce the heavy silence. *After how long the silence had dragged on, the shrill alarms were doing that well enough on their own*, she thought in annoyance and couldn't help glaring in the direction of the sound.

"We need to get back to our rooms," Blade said, his voice betraying none of the emotion from earlier.

Taking the cue from her team leader, Matrix raised some mental shields of her own. "We need to return the files to the safe," she said keeping any signs of panic out of her voice.

The two quickly moved to eject the hard drive from Blade's laptop when a file caught Matrix's eye. "Wait," she said catching Blade's hand.

"What?" he asked a hint of frantic annoyance tinting his voice. "That file," she indicated with a finger pointed at the screen, "open it." The file she had pointed to was larger than many of the others and recent. The title, "Project Marionette," had caught her attention because it was not related to the Phoenix program.

What they found inside was almost more disturbing than their last discovery. In the file were results from a device being tested, the device they, the Alpha team, had brought back from a mission a couple of months ago.

"This is bad," Matrix declared in a subdued tone laced with guilt. "This is Jamison's plan,"

Blade looked at her with troubled eyes, "and those men we captured, we delivered them right into his hands." "Download the file and then we need to get out of here.

It's not too late, we can stop this," Matrix said determinedly leaning over and giving his shoulder a firm squeeze.

Blade worked as quickly as possible to download all information referencing Project Marionette and the data from their past, then he ejected the hard drive. "Ok, time to move," he said standing to return the drive to its original location. Matrix gave him a firm nod, and the pair exited the room together, leaving no trace that they were there.

Dr. Jamison sat up in his quarters on the base. The alarms were blaring, and shouts could be heard from the hall. However, he merely stretched, yawning as he did so. The scientist calmly rose from his bed and changed into his day clothes. The Secretary of Defense was early he mused. His forces were not supposed to reach the base for a few hours. Oh well, his men were ready, and sleep could wait. Dr. Jamison couldn't repress a sigh as he exited his room and entered the chaotic hallway.

"Dr. Jamison, the troops are here!" a young man whose name he didn't know franticly shouted at him before running away.

Young recruits, they get worked up far too easily. Dr. Jamison simply continued to make his way toward his team's quarters.

In Washington, four men were meeting in a dark conference room. "You are sure this room is secure?" one of the shadowed figures asked.

"I have personally swept the room. No one will hear us," the man that moved from the back wall to the head of the table said, "And you are certain you were not followed?"

The first man's face could not be seen, but the annoyance was clear in his guttural response.

"Now gentlemen, let's not fight," a third voice spoke up.

"Of course, Senator," the Secretary of Defense said taking his seat in the low light that hung over the long table, "we were merely discussing security."

The director of the CIA scoffed at his sickeningly innocent tone but also took his seat to the right of the Secretary of Defense. As if the director of the CIA would have allowed himself to be followed.

Slowly, all four men took their seats, and the meeting began. "Now, you told me that you received the signal to send as many men as possible to the base," the Secretary of

Defense said looking to his right.

The three words that the CIA director spoke told them all they needed to know. "He is ready."

The large strike force that surrounded the top-secret base was hidden in the dense forest that surrounded the complex. Information on the base was limited, but they had enough men and women to take down at least five bases. Their orders were to overtake the base with as few casualties as possible. The eerie quiet that hung in the night and lack of activity was beginning to make the soldiers nervous. Once in position, men on all sides converged on the entrances simultaneously. They never knew what hit them. As soon as the doors opened, the men that entered began to fall and alarms began to sound.

Down in the lower levels of the base, all of the base's men were standing prepared for the invasion. Everyone's nerves were on edge as the awaited battle began. Orders were shouted and troops moved as the doors were opened. The teams of men that had planned to stealthily infiltrate the base had been expected and well prepared for. The first wave of soldiers went down quickly, and their unconscious bodies were dragged into large holding cells down below. Meanwhile, the remaining forces regrouped to try again.

Once back in her room, Matrix fell heavily to sit on her bed. Her thoughts were racing at a dizzying pace, and her pulse was not far behind. Blade had allowed her to hold onto the laptop containing the data they collected on Project Marionette, and she was currently holding onto it with enough force to threaten the structural integrity of the machine. It was going to take a while to process all the implications of the new information from the night's mission. However, it would appear that time was not going to be now. Evidently, Matrix and Blade had barely made it back to their rooms before Dr. Jamison arrived. Matrix had guessed that whatever was happening would be soon, and she was right.

Dr. Jamison strode into the secure hall where the children's rooms were located. "Wake up children," he announced through the comm system on the wall, "It's time to go to work."

The four children quickly readied themselves for whatever was to come next and entered the hall in under a minute. As Matrix and Blade exited their rooms, they shared a lingering glance. The betrayal still shone strongly in Blade's eyes as they met Matrix's, but none the less, he stood in line awaiting his instructions. If Dr. Jamison noticed the silent communication pass between the two, he chose not to comment.

Knowing the alarms would have already put them on alert, Dr. Jamison kept his instructions brief. "Our base is under attack," he told them, "I want you to go out there and bring them to their knees. But, many of them simply have not had the opportunity to see the light and will likely be joining us. Because of this, I want non-lethal force only. Is that clear?" he asked choosing to look directly at Ivy.

"Yes, sir," was the immediate response.

"Good, then you will be needing these," he smiled and extended a large black case of weapons. In the box were four stun guns, flash-bangs, tranquilizers, and sonic devices. Another box he presented also contained the team's signature weapons. As he extended his other hand to offer the second box, he issued another stern warning, "No lethal shots." Ivy nodded taking the box from him. His assessing gaze lingered on her, but evidentially, he decided to trust her and released his grip on the case. With one last glance over his team, he left to deal with other matters.

Each Phoenix took their share of the equipment and moved to grab their personal weapon. They had each been assigned at least one signature weapon that they demonstrated exceptional skill with and received extensive training to build on their natural prowess. Blade was first and grabbed his sniper rifle, throwing the sling over his shoulder. Next was Ivy who took out a katana. Someone seriously needed to address that girl's obsession with pointy objects. Following her was Corbet, he took several shurikens from the box and began to place them strategically around his body. Last was Matrix, her weapon was somewhat special and required an experienced hand. The weapon was a metal rod that was approximately two feet long, each end had electrified tips, and the center could screw apart to release a chain creating a futuristic nunchaku. Nunchaku required a considerable amount of focus to calculate how the strike would deflect the projected end back at the wielder, but none of them were your typical teenagers.

After gearing up, the team split up to cover the base. After giving the others a second to put some distance in between them, Matrix turned to Blade and pulled him around a corner. "Comms off" she mouthed to him.

Blade reached up to his ear and tapped the small device that was there and nodded.

"There is only one reason Jamison would want all of those men alive," she said, "He wants to use Project Marionette on them."

"That's what I'm afraid of," Blade concurred dejectedly, "What are we going to do?"

Matrix had been asking herself that same question since the first alarm sounded. "We cannot allow Jamison to amass this many troops," she said, "If we do, there will be no way of stopping him."

Blade nodded in agreement. "We will need to fight against our own," he said solemnly, and Matrix knew exactly who he was thinking about.

As team leader, Blade held a certain amount of responsibility for all four Phoenix team member's safety. The look on his face was pitiable, and Matrix gave him a tight smile in sympathy. Not that she liked the idea of fighting Corbet and Ivy either. They had all been used, but right now they couldn't risk bringing Corbet and Ivy into this fight without being able to show them the evidence they had seen. It was too big of a risk. They would have to hope that they could explain everything to them later.

"I know, but we don't have a choice," Matrix sighed.

She was halfway down the hall when Blade called out to stop her. "We should take them out first," he said almost sheepishly. It was a strange occurrence from him and under different circumstances, she might have teased their confident leader. She smiled at him, but there was no mirth in the expression.

"I've got Ivy," she said darkly, "Comms on, let's get into position."

Their rivalry was well known, and Blade almost protested, but Matrix had already disappeared around the corner Ivy had only minutes ago.

A minute after the two turned their comms back on, Corbet's voice sounded informing them that he was in position and a second later Ivy echoed him. "Beta team, hold your position until Alpha team is ready," Blade ordered.

"For the Alpha team, you guys sure are moving slow," Corbet jabbed with a short chuckle and another humorless laugh was heard across the line.

"Just hold your position," Blade said not bothering to cover the annoyance in his voice.

Matrix carefully scanned her surroundings as she neared the entrance Ivy had headed toward. The trained special operative would be difficult to sneak up on, even when she was relaxed, and certainly deadly if confronted. They had both had the same training, so her only advantage was that Ivy would likely be expecting the threat to come from the other direction. The fact that Matrix spotted her at all was surprising. Matrix usually liked to position herself high, but with Ivy, she knew to look low. The access Ivy was guarding was in a loading bay and storage room. Crates were stacked high and in slight disarray. The assassin of the team had positioned herself slightly to the left of the large room, behind a row of crates. From there, she wasn't backed into a corner and had a clear view of the outside entrance as well as the entrance from within the base. Fortunately, for the moment her attention was fixed on the outside entrance. Matrix took the opportunity to enter the room before she could be noticed. Like a shadow, she soundlessly glided into the room.

Ivy was watching the entrance ready for forces that were coordinating outside. The room was silent, but something caught her attention. It was like a sixth sense, she didn't know what had triggered it, but she found herself rising to turn and scan the room. Her eyes passed over her surroundings, but there was nothing in sight. She knew better than to ignore her instincts, but with no one in sight, she settled to resume her vigil. All the warning she had before an object impacted the side of her head was a dark shadow.

"I always knew you couldn't be trusted, Matrix," Ivy growled, stumbling back to her feet.

The two girls circled each other waiting for an opening. "It's not what you think, but I don't have the time to convince you," Matrix said, narrowing her eyes and slowing her pace, "so let's just get this over with."

Ivy scoffed, "I was never one for small talk anyway," she commented darkly.

With that, Ivy charged forward drawing her sword. Matrix nimbly sidestepped her attack, landing an elbow firmly into her back. The two girls spun to face each other again, but neither broke the agreed-upon silence. It was Matrix's turn to make the first move. She also pulled out her signature weapon and released the center chain. Her cross swing was easily avoided, but it had only been a distraction. As Ivy stepped in after the nunchaku passed, Matrix was prepared. Ivy attempted to pin her arm across her body, but Matrix landed a sidekick into her stomach that sent Ivy back trying to recover her balance. They had been sparring partners since they were children. Each knew the other's fighting style, but Matrix wasn't using her preferred fighting style. It would have been too predictable in this situation. The usually fierce and energetic fighter was taking a more calculated approach. Ivy smirked, clearly picking up on the difference. The next time, they both clashed in a tangle of punches and kicks. Both girls landed a series of blows on the other before breaking in a clash of shins. With the break, they took the opportunity to raise their weapons. They locked eyes for several seconds, each staring down the other.

Ivy had a split lip, Matrix's knuckles were bloodied, and both were assured an impressive collection of bruises tomorrow. Their rivalry ran deep, but Matrix decided it was time to end their dance. Matrix's next move was quick and efficient. Ivy was always the one to fight dirty, so the fire that ignited in her side took her slightly by surprise. It was more the suddenness than the pain that knocked her to her knees, but Matrix didn't hesitate to finish her with a strike to the back of her head with her nunchaku. Matrix took more satisfaction from that than she probably should have but couldn't help smiling as she slipped the stun gun back into her belt.

After Matrix finished binding Ivy's hands and feet, she gagged her and dragged the unconscious girl to the corner. Satisfied with her work, she strode toward the exit that led back into the base. "This is Black Phoenix, have you completed your objective?" she asked pressing a finger to her comm.

"Yes," Blade replied in person rounding the corner before Matrix. "I stunned Corbet in three seconds, what took you so long?" Blade asked in mock outrage.

Matrix stepped out of the way so he could see Ivy tied up on the floor and bloodied.

"You fought her," he said. It wasn't really a question; he had expected as much and didn't need to see Matrix's knuckles to confirm his assumption. A ghost of a smile flickered across Matrix's lips and Blade sighed. "Girls are disgusting," he joked with a disgusted expression.

"Yeah, they get blood everywhere," Matrix quickly fired back, a dangerous spark lighting up her eyes.

Blade only laughed. "Come on, we still have work to do."

CHAPTER 7

My Approach to Freedom

Outside the base, forces were preparing to mount a second attack when a young girl began approaching them from the base. "What is this kid doing?" one of the men asked under his breath. "Sir," he called to his commanding officer, "there is a girl approaching from the base." The man in charge raised his head from where he was checking his weapon to give the man a confused look.

"What?" was this guy trying to be funny, "Has she said anything? Could she have a bomb vest?" the commanding officer asked gravely.

"No, Sir, and I don't believe so, Sir," the man replied after considering the last question.

The girl was wearing a black, form-fitting uniform, it

was unlikely to be able to conceal a significant amount of explosives. She also did not appear to be in a hurry. Her strides were confident and deliberate, but her steps were those of someone coming to meet the other side, not attack them. However, she did appear to be well-armed. The man told his commanding officer everything he could make out about the girl, which was not much. The commanding officer gave a nod of acceptance then rose to meet the girl. If that truly was her intention.

Matrix knew she was taking a risk confronting the soldiers that were poised to attack the base, but it was possibly the only opportunity they would get to take down Jamison. She knew that Blade and herself alone would not be able to subdue the entire base designed to keep them in. Their only option was to hope that Matrix could convince the other side that they could trust her.

As Matrix approached the tree line that the strike team was occupying, she felt a surge of adrenalin pass through her body. Every soldier had a weapon fixed on her and it took calling on all of her past training to maintain a relaxed disposition. She needed to appear confident and in control, even if everything inside of her was screaming that she needed to take cover. Matrix breathed in a deep controlled breath and confidently forged ahead until she was standing face to face with the men on the front line. "I have a proposition," she stated calmly and clearly, "Who is in command here?"

The man she had approach stood blinking at her like he was being spoken to by some kind of unknown entity. Matrix simply held his gaze and waited for the man to find his words, but fortunately, another man approaching made the wait unnecessary. The tall, muscular commanding officer slowly stepped forward from the group. His striking, dark brown eyes appeared as though they were trying to pierce her soul as his gaze ran over her features. "Who are you?" he asked skeptically, his body remaining rigid in a defensive stance.

Ok, not a warm welcome, but she didn't expect this to be easy. At least he hadn't shot her. That she could work with. Dialing up the charming demeanor and slipping into character, Matrix prepared to make the sales pitch of her life. "My name is Matrix Cross," she answered coolly, "and we don't have time for pleasantries."

The man standing in front of her practically radiated strength. He looked to be in his forties, but his body was that of someone much younger. The way he carried himself spoke of a lifelong military man. His type usually responded best to the simple facts, no need to dance around the issue. "The man in that base is expecting you. Any attempt at infiltration will be met with strong resistance," Matrix began, "I can get your men inside, but you have to trust me. And, I need to know your orders."

Having served in the military since he was eighteen, Colonel Mike Redborn had been in a lot of unique positions, but a teenage girl that appeared to be a defector from a top-secret military base was new. Matrix waited patiently while the man considered her offer. Slowly and with great hesitance, the man began to nod. He didn't trust her, but if she said she could get his men inside, he was willing to listen.

Convincing the Colonel had not been easy, but with a bit of persuasion, they seemed to have formed a shaky alliance. Getting the man to outline his orders took more coaxing than asking a lion to hand over a fresh kill. At first,

Matrix was beginning to believe all it would accomplish was getting her hand bitten. In the end, Matrix decided not to tell the man that his orders came from someone under Jamison's control. It was clear that he didn't trust her, and she didn't believe it would gain her any favor. Matrix was rather surprised that the strike force had been ordered to infiltrate and destroy the base. She knew that it was only a cover to get the highly trained soldiers into the base and under Jamison's control. However, to avoid suspicions, Jamison's plants would have to make the operation appear legitimate she theorized. It made sense really, these men were not going to willingly submit themselves. Fortunately, Matrix could use that to her advantage and take down Jamison for real, with soldiers he supplied himself.

While Matrix went to confront the strike team sent to eliminate them, Blade cautiously made his way to the base's control center. The majority of the personnel were stationed in the lower levels where the soldiers were being lured and converted into Jamison's ranks. However, patrols were still making rounds to ensure the other side did not manage to get any scouts through undetected.

Blade was just peaking his head around the corner when he heard the rhythmic sound of boots on concrete. He quickly ducked into a conveniently placed maintenance room. A strong smell of cleaning products lingered in the air and he had to fight the urge to gag at the obnoxious smell. Blade held his breath for multiple reasons as he watched the two guards pass. He listened to the footsteps gradually fade away, and once he was certain they would not hear the door open; he grasped the metal knob and exited the relative safety of the closet. If Matrix was successful in convincing the strike team to work with them, it would be up to Blade to take down the alarms and video feeds as Matrix guided the soldiers in. With that goal in mind, Blade continued his progress toward the control center.

Blade knew that there was likely to be a large number of guards securing the room as well as the people monitoring the feeds. He usually preferred using a firearm, but under the circumstances, that was likely to draw unwanted attention before he could subdue the entire guard detail. Reaching into his vest pocket, Blade pulled out a weapon capable of incapacitating the entirety of the personnel simultaneously, one of the sonic devices that Jamison had given him. Under different circumstances, he might have even laughed at the irony, but his mind was currently too busy running through potential scenarios before engaging his former allies. But, were they ever truly allies? Or were he and his team merely weapons that needed to be controlled from the beginning? Shaking his head to clear his mind, Blade decided to stop that line of thought before anger could cloud his judgement. With a newfound determination, he inserted his hearing protection and tossed the sonic device around the corner. The effect was instant as the device impacted the floor. Even with his hearing protection, the shrill sound was uncomfortable, but it was effective. The guards standing outside of the control room fell to their knees with their hands over their ears. Taking advantage of their vulnerable position, Blade drew his tranquilizer gun and silently dropped three of the six guards before deciding to use a more physical method on the remaining three. He wasn't having a great day. Now, just the cyber people, *\this was almost too easy*, Blade thought with a smile. Jamison was too confident in his creations. He really should have put more thought into a contingency plan.

"Red Phoenix, this is Black Phoenix, the men are in position," Matrix's voice sounded over the commlink, "Have you secured the control room?" Her voice remained steady, even if it was slightly more tense than typical. They both knew that Jamison was likely monitoring their communications, so she was taking a risk speaking straight forward. However, it was likely that Jamison was already beginning to notice that something was not right, so she didn't have time for elaborate, coded communications. Matrix couldn't quite hold back a shaky exhale as Blade's clipped voice responded.

"Confirmed, control room is secure. Bringing down surveillance and alarms now. You are clear to move in." As he began disabling the base's systems, Blade couldn't help darting a satisfied smirk over his shoulder at one of the tied-up computer workers that was struggling in the corner. The man's muffled sounds that screamed displeasure only serving to earn him a deadly glare from the young asset.

"Alright Colonel, it's time to move," Matrix announced, relaying Blade's message. Matrix shrugged on the vest she had discarded before approaching the strike force and checked her weapons. With the men monitoring the surveillance system no longer giving updates, it would be crucial to move as quickly as possible before the base's guards figured out their plan. Matrix chose to enjoy the adrenaline rush rather than allow herself to be scared, but deep down she knew that the odds were greatly in favor of her regretting turning on someone with as much power as Jamison. Ha,

Jamison. Without realizing it, both her and Blade had dropped the title of "doctor" since learning that he had used them. The formal title once spoken with respect no longer seemed to fit the man, and she briefly wondered if Blade felt the same. She was beginning to look forward to bringing the former father figure to his knees. With that thought for motivation, Matrix began to lead the strike force to the loading bay where she had fought Ivy earlier.

With the surveillance cameras down, the team elected to move with speed rather than stealth before any of the guards on the base would have time to mobilize. The plan was simple, take out anyone who was not part of the strike force. The only complicating factor would be if Jamison had already begun converting the first wave of soldiers from the strike team's initial attack. Somehow Colonel Redborn did not seem like the type of man who would be willing to eliminate his own men. Frankly, Colonel Redborn was the only reason she didn't already have the entire base set to explode. Matrix had tried to explain Project Marionette to him and that the men he would be facing were no longer the men he had served with, but it proved to be a futile task. So, reluctantly, Matrix had agreed to help rescue those who had been captured.

Fully staffed, the military research base was designed to accommodate three hundred military personnel and scientists. Currently, there were two hundred fifteen military men station there and twenty scientists. The strike force sent to take the base had originally begun with seventy men, but the forces had already been cut down to fifty by their first attempt. Some of the guards would have to watch over the prisoners, so that left them at roughly a four to one disadvantage. But, with Blade in the control room, they would have the tactical advantage.

Before entering the base, Matrix peered through the loading bay doors to clear the room before the others could be seen. With no one in sight, she silently motioned them to follow her inside. Before moving into position, she had outlined the layout of the base, and they had determined who would break off into teams. Everyone smoothly broke off into five groups. Matrix joined Colonel Redborn's team to lead them down to where his men were being held.

Down below, Dr. Jamison had indeed realized that something was wrong. He could no longer access the surveillance feed, and the men in the control room had stopped sending updates and did not answer any attempts to contact them. The doctor let out a strangled cry of frustration and heavily slammed his fists against a desk. The sudden outburst startled many of the other scientists. Up until now, he had been the picture of calm and composure. But, as Dr. Jamison went on to forcefully sweep the contents of the desk to the floor, the entire room subconsciously took a step back. The doctor furiously turned to the guards stationed at that door muttering a few thankfully unintelligible, angry words under his breath.

The guards straightened at the expression of the angry man and did not hesitate to leave when he loudly told them to go find out what the heck was going on.

Dr. Jamison knew that this was undoubtedly the result of enemy soldiers infiltrating the base, but how would they have made it inside undetected? They had minimal intel on the base. The men, his men, who sent them had made sure of that. They had to have gotten help, but from whom?

"Black Phoenix, four-man patrol around the next corner," Blade informed over the comms.

The base consisted of four levels, two above ground and two below. The strike force entered on the first ground floor. The old base had been renovated many times over the years and was beginning to look a bit thrown together. As one moved through the levels, it was like moving back in time. The second level was the newest part of the building and had been added during the most recent renovation. It was constructed after the purpose of the base shifted to research. The ground floor was part of the original base but had been renovated and added onto the most over the years. One of those additions included the training facilities for the Phoenix team and their holding rooms. The first subterranean level had not undergone significant reconstruction but was still significantly used. It primarily served as the housing level for the base's staff. Being underground offered the personnel a small amount of protection if the base was ever attacked. The final level had not been renovated since the construction of the base in 1902 and there were no records of it being used in the last forty years.

There had been no sign of anyone other than a few sparse patrols on the ground floor, so it was likely that Jamison was trying to draw his enemy down below. Matrix and one of the members of her team, whose name she didn't know, quickly took out the four-man patrol. It was smart, really. If Jamison could funnel the teams down the stairwells, he could pick them off as they exited. There were nearly two hundred men waiting for them, and Jamison's men had the advantage of knowing the base.

While looking over the file for Project Marionette, there were records of the experiments performed on the Secretary of Defense, director of the CIA, the Speaker of the House, and the Senator. Matrix knew that they were taken to the lower levels of the base, but the personnel's quarters would not have the equipment or space necessary for the tests. The only logical conclusion was that Jamison has been using the second subterranean level. That would explain how he had managed to hide his work from the supervisors sent by the government. To their knowledge, the lowest level was no longer in use.

Matrix and the team were almost to the closest stairwell when Matrix stopped them. "Wait," Matrix whispered to Colonel Redborn, "the stairwell will be heavily guarded. I have another way down."

When the base was constructed, an emergency access was constructed to reach the lower levels. When they were younger, the children of the Phoenix program would sometimes sneak out and explore the base and the surrounding area after dark. Matrix discovered the access shaft when she was eight... and was almost shot by one of the guards while attempting to unseal the passage. Not the time to think about potentially getting shot she mused, but the access would be the perfect way to get past the guards undetected.

"Red Phoenix?" she asked pressing a finger to her ear, "Can you guide us the best way to that sublevel access we found November second, 1997?"

"Of course," Blade said smiling at the monitors, "make a right at the end of the hallway, it's clear."

CHAPTER 8

Never Threaten Me

D r. Jamison was pacing the lab. It had been too long since the first attack, and the two guards he sent never returned. Suddenly, a frantic man burst through the door. "Sir, we just lost contact with the last patrol. It seems they have split up to descend from all directions," the young soldier quickly spilled out, panting heavily.

Having regained his composure from earlier, Dr. Jamison locked onto the young man with a steady gaze. "We are prepared for them," he stated, "tell the men to hold steady for now. Let them come to us."

Nodding anxiously, the young man turned to report back to whoever had sent him.

It was only a minute after the young soldier had left that

gunfire could be heard from the level above. Dr. Jamison shifted his eyes upward in an attempt to determine what direction the shots were coming from. He spun slowly in a circle before his suspicions were confirmed by one of the other scientists.

"I think they are attacking from all four corners," Dr. Parkins, one of Dr. Jamison's trusted team members said to him nervously.

"This is all part of the plan," Dr. Jamison reminded him, "They will never be able to penetrate our greater forces." Dr. Parkins nodded in reluctant agreement, but his entire body still screamed tension and fear. "I am going to go up and see how our guardians are doing," Dr. Jamison said with an impressive mix of sarcasm, humor, as well as a touch of genuine concern. His intention was to lighten the mood, but he could not quite bring himself to compliment the unrefined imbeciles he was forced to rely upon. Before Dr. Jamison left, he turned to give his colleagues a reassuring expression, but he couldn't help the evil smile that twisted his face as he saw the twenty sedated bodies laid out on the floor behind them. In the end, it would all be worth it he assured himself.

In the meantime, Matrix and her new team were descending the ladder to the lowest level of the base. Matrix jumped, skipping the last five rungs of the ladder to land nimbly facing the other direction with her weapon raised. The area of the subterranean level they entered at was dark and did not appear to have been occupied in the last few decades. Still, she pulled a small flashlight from her belt and scanned as far as she could see with the narrow beam of light.

The emergency access let them out in the back-left corner of the base, at a junction of two perpendicular hallways. The walls were the same dull gray as the rest of the original building, with the exception of a water line approximately halfway between the floor and the low ceiling, indicating flooding at some point in the base's history. But, with nothing to indicate danger, aside from the musty smell that likely spoke of mold and mildew, Matrix called up "clear" to the team waiting for the signal to join her.

Colonel Redborn dropped down first to land beside Matrix. The look of disgust on his face was priceless, but to his credit, the man managed to suppress the groan that threatened to break his professional, command disposition. "Now, where are my men?" the Colonel demanded, turning to loom over Matrix threateningly.

Casually sidestepping the man, she moved to a more comfortable distance before answering him. "I don't know, Colonel," she replied, punctuating each word, "I was never permitted on this level. This is a large base, and it would have been foolish to assume that we would descend into the exact room that your men are being held in." Wow, that was sassy, Matrix thought to herself. If she had ever spoken to a superior like that under Jamison's control, she would have been tenaciously flogged. But it was necessary to ensure that she maintained an equal position with this man, a difficult task considering he was still looking at her like a child. Gaining his respect by standing up to him was perhaps the most efficient way to accomplish that task. Her role is to read people on missions, and this man was turning out to be a large print, first edition screaming to be read. He may be an excellent soldier, but his superior better not send him on a delicate undercover mission. Ever.

The staring contest that ensued stretched on for an

agonizingly long time before the Colonel seemed to decide that he still needed her. "Which way then?" he asked without breaking eye contact.

Matrix held his gaze for a few more tense seconds before dropping her head to the right and bringing a hand to her ear. "Black Phoenix to Red Phoenix, do you still have our location?" Matrix asked pressing on the earpiece. Matrix waited a couple of seconds but was rewarded with nothing but silence. "Black Phoenix to Red Phoenix, do you copy?" she tried again. Still nothing, great. "We must be too deep," she surmised out loud, "Our comms have limited range, the signal must not be able to penetrate this far underground. We are going to be on our own down here."

"Convenient," one of the members of the team whispered challengingly behind her, to which she responded with a withering glare.

However, Colonel Redborn nodded, albeit reluctantly. "Which way do we go?" he asked.

Matrix considered the question for a moment. Honestly, she had no way of knowing, but saying as much would diminish her credibility and possibly her usefulness in the Colonel's eyes. However, it would diminish her credibility considerably more if she were to lead them in the wrong direction.

The odds were in favor of the lab being closer to the power station like the ones on the ground floor, but it was also possible that Dr. Jamison selected a location for his experiment based on the most strategically defendable position or even the most conveniently located. There were too many variables to definitively say where the men were being held.

Matrix took a deep breath and did her best to appear confident before answering Colonel Redborn. "As I said before, I have never been allowed down here, so I do not know," she began honestly and matter-of-factly. "But, I told you I would lead you to your men," she added quickly, prompted by the Colonel's displeased expression. In addition, Matrix raised her hands in a pacifying gesture before continuing, "I believe that logically, the lab where your men are being held will be that way," she concluded and moved her hand to indicate the hallway behind the Colonel.

Colonel Redborn gave another one of his signature evaluating stares before finally accepting the answer she had given him. "I will lead the way," he stated, and it definitely was not an offer.

Matrix was about to protest, but the Colonel cut her off before she could begin. "My team has the better lighting equipment, so it is logical that one of us should take the lead," he said in a surprising display of rational thinking. But Matrix barely had time to be content with that before he added sarcastically, "And I'm sure you, Princess Practical, should be able to deal with that."

This was going to be a long operation. The team she normally worked with, the Phoenix Team, had worked together since they were very young, and they knew each other well. It had been a long time since Matrix had to work with someone on the same team as her who did not want to trust her. Even Ivy trusted her to do her job on a mission.

The newly formed team continued down through the damp, dark underground corridors, turning at Matrix's command. There had yet to be any sign of life, but suddenly Matrix stopped.

"What is the meaning of this?" Colonel Redborn asked in outrage and turned to level his firearm on the girl.

Matrix, unfazed, threw a look over her shoulder and

shushed the angry man. "We have been following you blindly through hallways without question. Tell me why we have stopped here, or I am ending this charade now," the Colonel exclaimed, moving the gun closer.

With an exasperated sigh, Matrix turned to fully face the man. With her body squared toward him, the gun was now planted firmly in her chest, but she gave away no sign of distress. "I heard gunshots, your men are advancing against the base's army," Matrix explained coolly and brought her hands up to her sides. Then, in one swift movement, she brought her hands together from opposite directions across the Colonel's forearm and wrist. With practiced ease, she maneuvered the gun from his hands and turned it to face his wide eyes, all before he could blink.

Loyally, the other members of the strike force under Colonel Redborn's command raised their weapons to point at Matrix, but she didn't waver. "Never threaten me again," her voice was cool, but the message was clear.

The Colonel was seeing her in a different light, down the barrel of a forty-five, and for once, he was not seeing her as a child. Nodding he raised his hands, palms down, to his team, "Everyone, let's just relax and put the guns down." Reluctantly, his men complied, but Matrix was not quite finished making her point and remained in stance. The gunshots above were becoming much more frequent and only raising the tension in the atmosphere.

"I need to know that you are not going to flip sides on me every time you get a little nervous," the question, *do you trust me?* was left unspoken, but the Colonel understood her meaning all the same and replied accordingly.

"I am willing to trust you, but first I need my gun back," he said cautiously. In reality, he didn't know if he would ever trust Matrix, but he still needed her to find his men before this Dr. Jamison could do... whatever it is he intends to do with them.

It was Matrix's turn to scrutinize the Colonel, but she knew that she needed him as well. Eventually, with deliberate movements, she ejected the magazine from the handgun, wracked the slide to remove the bullet in the chamber, caught that bullet, and finally returned it all to the original owner. The relief was clear on the Colonel's face, along with a considerable amount of annoyance as he reloaded his weapon. Their shaky truce had been reestablished, but Matrix had her doubts about its ability to last.

As Dr. Jamison exited the lift to the level above, he entered a deserted hall. The gunshots had faded into silence, leaving nothing to show that their startling sound had existed outside of his imagination. The only sounds he could hear were the increased rate of his heart and the sound of his restrained breaths. But with no danger in sight, Dr. Jamison cautiously made his way down the hall in search of someone to update him on the situation. The stairwells to the lowest level of the base had been sealed off to prevent the enemy soldiers from bypassing his forces and reaching the lab. This left only one way to reach the level above. Dr. Jamison had chosen the lift located in the center of the base to avoid the teams of men that were attacking from the stairwells, but this meant that he would have to walk quite a distance to reach one of the four corners where his men would be defending.

Dr. Jamison's entire body was tense as he cautiously traversed the dimly lit corridors. He had almost made it to the door that his men were stationed behind when a deafening blast erupted behind the metal barrier. The painful silence that followed was instantly filled by painful voices, some men were screaming, others were yelling out orders over the chaos. Dr. Jamison hesitated a moment, debating whether or not he should go in, but eventually, he gathered his resolve and opened the door. The old metal door creaked as the handle gave way and the hinges rotated. A plume of smoke rose through the open airway eliciting a small cough from the doctor. Inside the space, men were quickly moving, the gunfire had begun in the stairwell again, and injured men were being carried away from the destruction, but Dr. Jamison managed to find a familiar face through the smoke and bustle.

"Major Baker," the doctor called over the commotion. A muscular man with a mustache approximately in his mid-thirties looked up from a tense discussion with two lower ranks to find the man who had called his name. After spotting his superior, Major Baker dismissed the two men and cut through the room to reach the doctor.

Upon reaching Dr. Jamison, he snapped to attention, "Major Tyrone Baker, Sir."

"Situation report," Dr. Jamison demanded.

"The enemy has thrown a powerful explosive device down the stairs, we have ten wounded," the Major dutifully reported.

"Prior to that?" the doctor prompted him to continue.

"The enemy has been unable to bypass our men. We incapacitated several of their men in the first round of fire. However, we were unable to recover them for the cause. Up until moments ago, they appeared to be strategizing to try again," Major Baker reported. "I suppose the bomb was what they came up with," he added, "They attempted to use the explosion to gain ground, but my men are holding them off. Without cover in the stairwell, they will likely be forced to retreat again."

Dr. Jamison nodded in understanding, absently dismissing the Major to return to his job. Major Baker saluted and eagerly returned to his men.

Dr. Jamison had learned all he needed to know. His men greatly outnumber the enemy, but his men in Washington had sent him the best. Retrieving them was proving to be a challenge he mused. Dr. Jamison's thoughts were heavily occupied as he made the return trip to the lift. He slowly extended his hand to the down arrow only to stop short. They recovered twenty highly trained men in the first assault, perhaps it was time to start replenishing his ranks with more... refined soldiers.

CHAPTER 9

Project Marionette

"If I'm correct, Dr. Jamison's lab should be through those doors," Matrix said with a hint of nervous energy finding its way into her voice. The stressful trip through the abandoned section of the lowest level of the base had finally led them to what Matrix hoped would be the location Dr. Jamison chose to perform his less than ethical, unsanctioned experiments. A set of heavily rusted metal doors was all that stood between them and whatever security measures Dr. Jamison put in place. The solid design of the doors gave away no hint as to what awaited them on the other side.

"Well, what are we waiting for?" Colonel Redborn asked pointing at the doors with his rifle.

Matrix had to repress the sigh that threatened to break

her calm exterior. "We need to be smart about this, Jamison will likely have the prisoners under heavy guard," Matrix chose to leave out that the odds of his men still being his men were already extremely low.

"You have done your part, child, but now it is time for me to get my men back. "Step aside," he ordered.

For someone selected to lead a highly trained group of men to take down an entire military research base, the Colonel was proving to be a highly impulsive man. Perhaps his personality would be better suited to following orders than making command decisions. The Colonel's ill-fitting role did not go unnoticed by Matrix, and it was clear to her that this man being selected to lead the team had not been by chance. Dr. Jamison's men in Washington clearly had a lot of influence to be able to control who led the attack on the base. And they obviously did not want the mission to be successful.

Reluctantly, Matrix moved out of the Colonel's way. "What is your plan?" she asked.

Colonel Redborn paused for a moment before turning to his team. Gesturing to five of the men, he instructed them to take the right side of the room and the other half to follow him to the left. After that, he turned to Matrix and with a threatening tone warned her to stay out of his way.

"Carson, get up here," the Colonel ordered. A petite brunette with her hair pulled back into a smooth ponytail scrambled up to Colonel Redborn. "You carrying a charge?" he asked.

"Yes sir," the brunette responded enthusiastically.

A bit too enthusiastically Matrix noted. The last variable she needed to add to this equation would be a pyromaniac. However, the Colonel did not seem concerned.

"Very good, would you please do the honor of opening

the door for us, Lieutenant," he said with a smile. Lieutenant Carson eagerly made her way to the doors and attached a small device. "Everyone might want to take a few steps back," she advised, walking back to a safe distance herself.

Taking their cue from the Lieutenant, the rest of the team backed up just behind where Carson stopped. Colonel Redborn took his position at the front of the men on the left side of the hall. The Colonel lifted his gaze across the hall to where the Lieutenant was looking at him and holding the remote trigger. Raising his right hand above his head, he held up three fingers and the Lieutenant nodded. Several of the men shifted anxiously raising their weapons as one of his fingers fell. Lieutenant Carson's eyes did not blink as she watched until the last finger was remaining. Turning her attention to the doors ahead, she pressed the trigger. The explosion was instantaneous, and everyone raised their arms to shield themselves from the debris. Before the smoke managed to settle, the team stormed the room to confront whatever was waiting for them inside.

Above them, Dr. Jamison's men had regained the upper hand. After the explosion in the stairwell, the strike force managed to push forward slightly but their progress quickly stalled. The explosion took out several of Dr. Jamison's men, but with their greater numbers, the defending side was in position to pick off anyone who advanced any further.

Matrix almost wished she had been wrong about the location of the lab. The moment they had come through the doors they were met with resistance, but it was not the guards that froze the team. Behind the door was a wide, fully lit hall leading straight ahead to a large laboratory filled with scientists. The resistance consisted of five stunned guards that were easily taken out and several terrified scientists that were held at gunpoint. After confirming that the threat had been eliminated, the team spread out to search the room. Most of the soldiers moved to check the rest of the entrances to the room, while Matrix approached a locked room connected to the lab.

Colonel Redborn noticed her break from the rest of the group and moved to follow her. "Do you know what's in there?" he asked.

"I'm not certain," she replied, genuinely hoping that she didn't. Matrix reached for a lock pick set in her belt and pulled out the proper pick and torsion wrench. She kneeled in front of the door and inserted her tools into the old-fashioned lock and felt for the familiar clicks as the lock gave way. Matrix held her hand on the handle and looked up to Colonel Redborn who raised his gun and nodded. Matrix threw the door open and jumped back, drawing her weapon in the process.

The five men strapped into chairs is what froze the team. Drawn over by their team leader's gasp, the entire team looked in on the men that had been waiting in the tree line with them only a few hours ago.

"This is Project Marionette?" the Colonel asked.

He hadn't known what to expect when Matrix told him that his men would be converted against him by a device. Frankly, he had not believed her, certainly not any more than he trusted her. But seeing his men strapped down with tubes and wires spiraling from their bodies, wires that were connected to some kind of machine, well, it made it harder for his mind to deny.

Matrix was the first to break the silence, unfazed by the scene. "It would appear they have already converted the rest of your men," she said solemnly, but matter-of-factly. She had hoped to be able to free the Colonel's men, but that was no longer possible. She was trained to not become attached to those she worked with, and now she was being forced to rely on someone who did not appear to have been taught the same separation.

Matrix glanced around the room until her eyes landed on a small device sitting on top of one of the machines. She purposefully strode over to the device but stopped short of touching it. Her eyes scanned over the device, carefully assessing the situation. The metal sphere was sitting securely in a metal ring that served as a cradle. There were numerous wires connected to the device through a panel on the bottom. Matrix's attention was drawn to the wires, but none of them seemed to be connected to any kind of pressure sensor or other security measures. With steady hands, she cautiously probed the device running her fingers along the many groves, buttons, and switches. A faint blue light emitted from the groves that ran haphazardly around the sphere indicating that it had been activated. To her surprise, the metal was quite hot. Matrix did not see how many of Colonel Redborn's men had been taken in the first attack, but based on the temperature of the device, it had been in use for a while.

"How does it work?" the Colonel asked without taking his eyes off his men.

Matrix straightened, shifting her attention away from the glowing sphere. "Colonel..." she began to placate, but he did not give her the chance to explain that it would be pointless to go into detail on the complicated process, especially now.

"I need to know," he stressed through gritted teeth.

For a moment it was almost painful to see someone who openly cared for their team. Matrix had to force her mind away from the concept, but she decided to cave in to the man's request. There had been very little time to study the device when she and Blade came across it in Dr. Jamison's office, and she barely had time to open the file before Jamison came to get the team. Truthfully, she didn't know exactly how the device worked, but perhaps she could satisfy Colonel Redborn with a basic description. Ha, if she ever gave Jamison anything less than the exact report down to the final detail... well her mind didn't want to go there either.

"Basically, the device is capable of emitting a pulse that can be manipulated to cause the brain to "block" past memories. During this time the subject was found to be highly impressionable, to the extent that the scientists could reshape the entire past of the subject through suggestion and programming techniques," Matrix began to paraphrase the basic idea of what she had read.

Already the Colonel's face had begun to twist into an expression of anger and confusion. His hands were clenched into tight fists and his eyes fixed unseeing on his men, but Matrix continued. "The discovery was an accident. It was theorized by the scientist originally working on the device in the '60s that it activated the part of the mind that blocks traumatic memories or possibly was even breaking down the neural pathways that stored those memories. There were never any experiments performed attempting to reverse the effects, and after the project was shut down, no further research was conducted. Your men are gone, Colonel." "I'm sorry," she added softly to conclude her lecture.

Matrix's eyes stayed trained on the Colonel while he processed the information she had given him. Matrix was silently hoping that he would accept her assessment and move on with the mission, but she did not need her body language training to read the Colonel. Anger was radiating off the man in waves. Colonel Redborn walked over to one of the machines and slammed his fist down sending electronic pieces flying and tools clattering to the ground. An anguished scream tore its way out of his lungs, and he dropped his head to his hands. Twenty men, he lost twenty men to that monster. In his despair, Colonel Redborn did not sense the person coming up behind him. The reaction had been almost instant after the Colonel's outburst. The men strapped to the chairs ripped off their restraints and jumped up to attack their former allies.

Matrix dove under the man who had thrown himself at her. She slid over to the machine and jumped snatching the device from its cradle. Matrix rolled, turning her body away from the machine to shield herself from the consequences of removing the device. She braced herself with her eyes closed, but nothing happened. Surprised, she turned back to the machine the device had been connected to. Clearly, Jamison had not been expecting anyone to make it to the lowest level, she thought slightly puzzled. She had been prepared for whatever defense mechanism Jamison would have had tied into the machine, but there was no explosion or even an alarm.

Earlier, after Dr. Jamison had come back from talking with Major Baker, the doctor exited the lift determined to begin the conversion of the latest additions to his army.

"Dr. Parkins," Dr. Jamison greeted as he entered the lab. Once in the room, Dr. Jamison made his way over to the men on the floor. The eyes of the other scientists followed him anxiously awaiting news from above. But, he gave no indication that any such report would be forthcoming. Having been addressed by Dr. Jamison, Dr. Parkins followed Jamison to the back of the lab where the men were lying. Hesitantly, he walked up behind the doctor. Dr. Jamison was bent over one of the soldiers checking his vital signs, seemingly oblivious to the man behind him.

Dr. Parkins lightly cleared his throat, catching the doctor's attention. Dr. Jamison rose steadily and turned to look at him. Dr. Parkins shifted uncomfortably under Jamison's scrutinizing eyes. They remained that way for an uncomfortably long time before Dr. Parkins dared to break the silence. "Was... was there any news from the Major, sir?" he asked cautiously.

Dr. Jamison continued to lock eyes with the man, but Dr. Parkins was unable to sustain eye contact. His gaze continued to nervously dart around the room, his eyes only landing on Dr. Jamison's a second before flittering off.

Once Dr. Jamison decided that the man had had enough and his message was clear, he simply turned to the others. "We are beginning conversion immediately," he informed them. The other scientists traded meaningful looks before one of them finally spoke up.

"Sir, to properly convert the men will take time," the scientist reminded him.

Dr. Jamison turned his full attention to the man challenging him. The comment earned the scientist a venomous glare. "I don't need them all to have full backstories, I just need them to be compliant," Dr. Jamison bit back. He was not going to allow his own men to challenge him.

"Their loyalty may not be as strong without proper

justification in their minds," the other doctor continued to point out.

"This is your last warning, Dr. Moretti. Get to work," after that order, Dr. Jamison turned and began prepping his first subject.

Quicker than expected, the process was almost complete. With Marionette already used on seventy-five percent of the men, Dr. Jamison decided it was time to check on his men upstairs again. "Finish with the rest," he told his team, "I am going to check in with Major Baker."

It was shortly after this that Matrix and the strike team had broken through the doors.

Back in the present time, Matrix was standing up to examine the machine she had pulled the device from. There were no obvious signs that removing the device had triggered any kind of security measures, but she had very little time to investigate before one of Jamison's newest goons came up behind her.

The man threw his arms around Matrix and lifted her feet from the ground. An easy feat considering that he was nearly a foot taller than the girl. Matrix retaliated with several hard elbows to the man's ribs, smirking when she felt a familiar crunch after the final blow connected. Instinctually the man released her, drawing an arm protectively around his offended midsection. When her feet were back on the ground, Matrix spun not hesitating to kick the man in the nose. The man stumbled back a couple of steps before raising his head to lock eyes with Matrix. Blood had begun flowing from his nose, but there was no indication that he even noticed. His deep brown eyes stared into her electric blue ones through an unseeing haze, the unfocussed gazed briefly catching Matrix off guard. Perhaps it was the concussion Matrix had undoubtedly just given the man, but it was as if she were staring into the eyes of a robot. There was no emotion, no pain, nothing, just a body ready to fight. Maybe this is what it was like to fight her? However, her thoughts didn't linger. Matrix quickly recovered to move in and finish the man. The fight was brief, and the result was predictable.

Turning away from the man on the floor, Matrix sought to locate Colonel Redborn. She had absently noticed the man go down as she scrambled to secure the device. Now looking out over the chaos of the room, she found him struggling to pin one of his former allies to the floor. Matrix quickly moved to help the struggling man. Colonel Redborn was desperately and futilely trying to negotiate with his attacker, but he was in no position to hear the Colonel's pleas. With her stun gun drawn, Matrix ended the abortive, one-sided conversation by incapacitating the offending man without remorse.

"These are not your men anymore, Colonel," she reminded him, "You cannot treat them as such."

Colonel Redborn sent her a dangerous glare that she mirrored back at him.

"We need to end this quickly and quietly," Matrix stressed.

As if on cue, one of the men fired his gun. A single shot and the entire room went silent. The five converted men were down, but they all knew that that shot would draw more men down.

"Jennings!" Colonel Redborn reprimanded his man and the room broke into a heated argument. Some were angry that one of their comrades had been shot, others because their cover had been blown, and the Colonel it seemed just wanted to yell at someone.

Ignoring the others, Matrix walked back into the main lab with quick, powerful strides. It was futile to discuss the shot at this point. Preparing for the men that would be sent in response should be top priority, so Matrix took her position and waited.

Things were going well for Dr. Jamison and his men. "Our forces outnumber them. They can't hold out forever. It's just a matter of time," Major Baker told Dr. Jamison confidently.

"Very good, Major," Dr. Jamison praised, "I will inform my team. I'm sure they will be pleased to hear it." Dr. Jamison turned to return to his lab but stopped to add one last amendment to the Major's orders. "Oh, Major Baker," he began, causing the man to turn back to him, "tell your men if they see one of the Phoenixes, no kill shots, but bring them to me."

The Major was slightly taken back by this but nodded dutifully. Satisfied, Dr. Jamison began his trek to the lift.

As Dr. Jamison neared the lift, the gunfire faded to a dull, muffled hum in the background. Sighing wearily, he made the final turn to face the lift. The gunshot that rang out below him took the doctor completely by surprise. The man froze as a streak of panic shot through his body. Every nerve went on high alert, and his senses went into overdrive. The strike force couldn't have made it below. It shouldn't be possible. Shaking himself out of the shock, Dr. Jamison turned to run back to the Major. His heart was pounding in his ears, and he arrived back too out of breath to speak. Everything had been going so well, how did they make it to the lab? Could it be his own men? Dr. Jamison took several deep breaths to compose himself and pushed through the doors to find Major Baker again.

Quickly spotting the tall, dark man, Dr. Jamison called out to the Major. An expression of confusion flickered across the Major's face but was quickly hidden behind a mask of professionalism.

"What's wrong Dr. Jamison?" his baritone voice asked when he was close enough to see the doctor was out of breath.

"I need a team of your men to head to the lowest level, "Dr. Jamison panted out. "We have intruders," he announced gravely.

CHAPTER 10

The Price You Pay in Blood

The echoes of footsteps carried into the lab from the outer hall. The ominous thuds indicating a large group of men preparing to descend on Matrix and the still bickering imbeciles she had resorted to working with.

They were under the center of the base; the lift was probably the only access to the lowest level that would not have been sealed off. Judging by the distance to the lift, the amplitude and pattern of the steps, and when she first heard the steps, Matrix did a quick calculation. By her estimation, there were twenty men preparing to converge on the lab. With her frustration reaching its limit, Matrix turned to the room behind her. "Enough!" she practically screamed at them. But it had the desired effect. Everyone in the room was now looking at her. She let the awkward silence left by the sudden drop in the bickering linger for a moment before speaking. "We have twenty hostiles incoming. I suggest we meet them with force," she informed them with a much softer tone, then turned to resume her vigil.

The echo of footsteps grew louder, and the tension increased. The strike team had set their differences aside for the moment, and Matrix was grateful for the silence. The scientists tied and gaged in the corner were becoming restless, but an additional gun pointed their way served to silence the group.

The sound of the footsteps continued to build until they suddenly ceased. The air buzzed with nervous energy as the strike force waited for the other side to make their move. The sound of one individual's boots tapping against the ground signaled the approach of one of the soldiers. A young voice called to the scientists, "Doctors? Is everything alright? We received a report of gunfire from this area." He sounded nervous.

They are likely trying to make their team sound less threatening Matrix theorized.

The men holding their guns on the scientists eyed the group threateningly as the young man spoke. Their message was clear, make a sound, and we fire. Keeping their hostages quiet was essential. The less Jamison's men knew about them, the better their chances of success.

Matrix looked over at the Colonel. The man had his rifle aimed at the doorway but looked to Matrix when she caught his eye. There was no way to know how long a standoff would last and time was an issue. Their best chance was offense. With their hostages, Jamison's men would not be able to fire around the corner without risking hitting their own men. The two nodded at each other, better to move on the enemy before they expect it. With the team ready to move, Colonel Redborn gave the signal and the fight began.

Until this point, their objective had, for the most part, been stealth, but now the strike force flooded the hallway, overwhelming the enemy before they had time to react. Nearly the entire opposing force had been taken out before they were able to return fire. The few enemy soldiers that were able to avoid the first round of fire were outnumbered and quickly overpowered. Colonel Redborn moved to the front of the group, pushing past his men to clear the hall himself. Satisfied that the threat had been eliminated, he motioned for the rest of his team to follow.

Above them, Dr. Jamison and Major Baker were waiting for a report from the team sent to check the lab for intruders. "They will have made it to the lab by now," Major Baker absently spoke aloud.

Dr. Jamison nodded slightly in acknowledgement, too deep in thought for a more eloquent response. Everything had been going so well, his plan must succeed. How could they have gotten beneath them? And, he was not even sure what to believe about the Phoenix team anymore. All of this was for the Phoenix team, but something told him that he could not rely on them this time.

"Listen," Major Baker implored in an urgent whisper, breaking Dr. Jamison from his thoughts. The two men moved further down the halls leading to the center of the base and away from the gunfire in the stairwell. The two men stopped as soon as they were far enough away to distinguish rapid gunfire sounding from below them. The doctor and the major turned to look at each other in the eye.

Neither spoke, both unwilling to speculate what had transpired beneath them.

The gunfire only lasted a short time before it completely faded away. Dr. Jamison began to take a step forward, but Major Baker reached out a hand to stop him. Abruptly, Dr. Jamison spun to face the Major, eyeing the hand restraining him indignantly. "Perhaps it would be best if you waited here Doctor," Major Baker cautiously suggested.

The doctor appeared to be debating whether or not he was going to comply, so Major Baker thought it would be in his best interest to add to his case. "One of my men has orders to report back as soon as the team finds the cause of the first shot. He should be back soon, we just need to be patient for a bit," Major Baker bargained with the doctor.

Dr. Jamison continued to glare at him, but it seemed that he had made a strong enough case to prevent the doctor from rushing down the hall.

It was not that Dr. Jamison didn't believe the Major or that he thought it would be useful for him to run toward the gunfire, but right now he needed to do something. He hated not being in control, and right now he was not in his element. He was a scientist, not a soldier, and for the Major to tell him to be patient... All he has ever been is patient. That is why he had put his plan into motion in the first place. He spent years trying to convince the government to sanction his project, patiently working for approval. Then he patiently groomed his team from the time they were practically infants and now the government wanted to shut him down. No! He was done being patient. And now his team...

Just when the Major thought the doctor had settled down, Dr. Jamison ripped his arm from the Major's grip and marched down the hall. "I want every available man to follow me now!" Dr. Jamison barked out over his shoulder.

Matrix and the strike team did not notice the soldier that had slipped out to report back to the Major when the shooting started, but they already knew that they would have limited time before reinforcements came.

After Colonel Redborn cleared the hall, Matrix moved to the front to guide the team to the lift. Once they reached the lift, Matrix quickly called the car to prevent more of Jamison's men from coming down. When the doors opened, Matrix straddled the opening to prevent the doors from closing. "This is our only access to the levels above, and this is their only way down," Matrix informed the group.

"Great, then let them come. We'll pick them off as they exit," one of the men said confidently.

"That would be a great plan, but we can't do anything from down here and our men are outnumbered up there," Colonel Redborn pointed out. There was no way he was going to leave those men fighting while he sat comfortably in the basement.

"The Colonel is right, and if we wait much longer to go up, the second the lift's doors open, we will be the ones being picked off," Matrix voiced. Every second they waited reinforcements above would be getting closer.

"We have to go up," Colonel Redborn said resolutely and marched into the lift.

"Colonel, we have no way of knowing what will be waiting for us when those doors open. You lead these men, if you die, they will have no leader," Matrix said matter-of-factly, "Communications should work one level up. I highly recommend that you wait for the first group to report."

A loud ding is emitted by the elevator, and Matrix leans into the right door as it slides partially closed in an attempt to motivate her to move.

"I am not risking any more of my men than necessary."

*Ding!

"I am going up with the first group," Colonel Redborn argued back.

*Ding!

He had already lost so many...

*Ding!

There's no way he could back down now.

*Ding!

The faces of those men and women would haunt his dreams for the rest of his life.

*Ding!

And if that stupid elevator doesn't stop dinging...

*Ding!

It is going to meet the full force of his fury.

*Ding!

"That's it, I'm shooting it," Colonel Redborn decides in his mind. He is either going up now or he is blowing the thing to bits.

*Ding!

The Colonel emits a low growl of frustration. "In formation," he barks out to his men.

*Ding!

The group glances at each other briefly, and the men in the front begin to file into the lift. Matrix suppresses the urge to sigh and steps back into the lift with the strike force.

As the car roughly glides up the old shaft, one of the soldiers in the front, whose name Matrix has yet to learn, pulls two stun grenades out of his vest pockets. It was a risk to use them, if the enemy hasn't arrived yet, it will alert them that the strike team has and the stun grenades will only affect the strike team, but if Dr. Jamison's men have arrived, they will be eliminated as soon as the doors open.

The short ride up to the next level was tense. The nerves in the air were palpable in the small, tightly packed space. Including Matrix and the Colonel, there were ten people in the lift, all pressed against the sides for the little bit of shielding that the position would provide. Matrix, along with the rest of the team, covered their ears and squeezed their eyes tightly shut. The only exception was the soldier who stood ready at the doors, ready to deploy the two weapons.

The ride, while in reality only a few seconds, felt like an eternity. But the second the doors opened, the scene was thrust into motion. As the doors began to slowly crack, the soldier forced his way through to throw the stun grenades. One went to the left and one to the right, and the soldier pulled himself back into the car to take cover from the concussive blast.

The soldiers, currently led by Dr. Jamison himself, moving to intercept the strike force was nearing the lift.

Major Baker was following behind Dr. Jamison practically begging him to listen to reason and to go wait somewhere safe. But, Dr. Jamison continued to march forward with his eyes straight ahead, effectively tuning out the Major's pleading. The closer they got, the more insistent the Major became and the more determinedly the doctor ignored him. Finally, as they reached the last turn before the lift, the Major gave one last attempt to sway his leader. The

Major stopped where he was standing and yelled over the mass of soldiers that began to file around him. "You are going to get yourself killed!" he shouted, but the doctor marched on unfazed and the Major stood shaking his head.

It was just as the last of the force led by Dr. Jamison rounded the corner that the Major heard the deafening sound. Despite being the farthest away from the blast, Major Baker had to reach out a hand to the wall to prevent himself from falling as the compression wave hit him leaving him dizzy. His ears were ringing, and he had to squint to see as he stumbled to reach his men. The lift was only thirty feet from the corner, amplifying the effect of the device the Major recognized to be a stun grenade.

The men had been unprepared, but a few of the ones from the back had already begun to recover and move toward the lift with their weapons raised. However, the strike team had been prepared and took measures to shield themselves from the effect of the stun grenades as best they could.

Despite having their eyes and ears covered, the intense light and sound penetrated the meager cover of the lift. Matrix squinted into the light of the hallway attempting to readjust her eyes after the stimulus overload of the stun grenades. Her ears were ringing, but she fought through the muffled sounds of the impending battle to hear the Colonel yelling out orders to his men. She was one of the first to charge into the hallway followed closely by Colonel Redborn, and it appeared that their timing had been perfect. The enemy had not had sufficient time to set up a defense against the strike team and had encountered the stun grenades farther away from the lift, lessening the effects on the strike team. Dr. Jamison's team, however, had been at ground zero and suffered the full force of the detonation.

Major Baker saw the team filing out of the lift and realized that there was nothing he could do for his men now. The men that had staggered to their feet were already trying to take cover from the strike force, but the smooth-walled hallway of the base offered no shelter, so Major Baker ran.

The strike force used their advantage to skillfully and efficiently cut through the enemy resistance. As Colonel Redborn scanned the fallen men for any remaining threat, his eyes fell on the unconscious body of Dr. Jamison uncomfortably slumped against the wall to the left of the lift. The Colonel felt the anger rise in his chest at the sight of a man whose face he had only ever seen before in the files from his mission briefings. Silently, he hoped that the man was not dead. That would be too good for him. He made his way over to the doctor with slow, purposeful steps deciding what he would do with the man. First, he reached out a hand to check for a pulse. As his rough, calloused fingers brushed the man's skin he began to stir slightly. That was all the Colonel needed to know. Colonel Redborn roughly grabbed the doctor by the collar of his shirt and hauled him to his feet. "Open your eyes, you murderer!" he screamed in his face, shaking the doctor forcefully, the Colonel's hands snaking tighter around the doctor's neck.

Dr. Jamison's eyes opened wide with terror and his hands flew instinctively to his neck. The doctor began to flail, uselessly attempting to kick his attacker, but the Colonel held him in an iron grip born of hatred. "I-I... can offer... you the... highest... rank among my... men," Dr. Jamison managed to choke out through struggling breaths, but his offer was not met with enthusiasm.

Colonel Redborn eyed the doctor scrutinizing his words, then laughed. "Do you really think that I would join you after what you did to my men? I thought you were supposed to be a genius," the Colonel sneered, leaning in until their noses were almost touching.

Anger flashed through the doctor's eyes, but he seemed to think better of voicing his thoughts about this Paleolithic buffoon and tried to cower farther back from the angered colonel.

Seeing the fight bleed from the doctor almost disappointed the Colonel. He was hoping Dr. Jamison would put up a fight. It would have made this more satisfying. Colonel Redborn sighed wistfully, a one-sided fight would have to do. The Colonel began to push the doctor back, forcing his feet to scramble backward to alleviate the pressure on his neck. The Colonel continued to press the struggling man back until he was pinned against the wall. "You will pay for what you did to my men," Colonel Redborn spat in his face, and he had every intention of following through.

Colonel Redborn's men stood back several feet and watched unsympathetically as their commanding officer threw the defenseless doctor several feet into the other wall. Matrix watched with conflicted thoughts as she saw the Colonel begin to pummel her former mentor, but she could not bring herself to stop him. *Isolate your emotions*, you taught me that, she thought. For a while, she numbly observed the Colonel as he exacted his revenge, but she eventually turned and walked a short distance down the hall, not quite able to watch the man she once saw as a father be beaten to death.

As the blunt sounds of flesh on flesh began to die down, Matrix turned to rejoin the strike force. "Your men are waiting for us, let's move," she announced in a confident, but detached tone.

The Colonel slowly rose from his place over the doctor

on the floor and made his way over to Matrix. He walked with his head down and his arms hanging loosely by his sides like all the fight in him had left and had been replaced by mourning for his men. His uniform was torn and bloodied, his knuckles were raw, and the blood of his enemy dipped from his fingertips. But the most startling realization was a certain distance in his eyes that did not fit the passionate man but behind it, the anger still flickered like a flame waiting to be released again. As the Colonel moved away from the figure on the floor, Matrix couldn't help but catch a glimpse of the doctor's body. It was an image that would be burned into her mind for the rest of her life. His once white lab coat was a mangled mess of shredded material smeared red, his face was raw and swollen, and the blood gushed from an open laceration above his right eye.

Matrix stood frozen in time but drew her focus back up to the Colonel as the man came to stand before her. There was no remorse in his eyes, only pain, and Matrix briefly wondered if it was wise for him to continue leading the team in his current state of mind. But, Colonel Redborn surprised her. His command façade slipped back into place as he straightened his shoulders under Matrix's assessing gaze.

"Following your lead," he said with a quirk of his head and a hint of sarcasm bleeding into his voice.

Matrix nodded and assumed her place at the front of the strike team and began to guide them to the most critical staircase.

With the tension and commotion from the previous fight subsiding, Matrix was able to become more aware of her surroundings. In particular, a staticky voice in her ear.

The strike force had only made it a short distance through the base when Matrix stopped and raised a hand to her ear.

"What is it?" Colonel Redborn asked preparing for a fight.

Matrix raised her other hand up to Colonel to shush him.

"Ma-a-trix," the staticky voice repeated.

"Yes. Blade?" she asked hopefully.

"This... Red Phoen-..." Blade replied back over the comms, "I... h..ve... been t-trying... reach y-. The b-base's...f de...uct... be... trigg...d."

"Red Phoenix, you are breaking up. Please repeat," Matrix requested then turned to Colonel Redborn. "My teammate in the control room is trying to make contact, but we are still too far underground. The signal is weak," she informed him.

"Ba... self... uct ha... b... iggered. Rep...t, bas-s... s..lf... estr...t tri...erd," Blade tried to clearly repeat into the comms.

It only took a second for Matrix to decipher the message, and then the realization hit her. When she disconnected Project Marionette it triggered the base's self-destruct protocol. Dr. Jamison must have tied it into the device in case the strike force overtook the base, but he had not been planning on anyone being able to get past his men. That was his failsafe.

"Mat-trix, y... eed g..t... out," Blade urged her, "Ca...'t stop. Tw-we..ve min..."

"Acknowledged," Matrix responded, "I am going to recover the laptop." Matrix did not wait for his reply, she turned to the Colonel who was looking at her and clearly expecting an explanation. Matrix quickly briefed him on their situation, and he nodded thoughtfully. "I am going to recover the data my teammate and I secured last night," she then informed him. Earlier today? Had it really only been yesterday that everything had been normal? Absently she confirmed that her internal clock was accurate with a flick of her wrist. Seven o'clock on the minute, the sun would be rising now Matrix mentally noted. Returning to the present, Matrix began to instruct the strike force. "You now have eleven minutes to get out of here. Follow this hall until it ends, it will intersect another hallway turn left. That will take you to the main stairwell. They cannot defend against attackers from both sides. Once you overtake that stairwell, radio your men and tell them to get out," with her instructions complete, Matrix was already turning to leave.

Colonel Redborn was still processing everything that Matrix said when she turned to leave. From what he understood, this girl was Jamison's creation. There was no way he could trust Matrix to go off on her own knowing his plans, for all he knew, she could be sending them into a trap. Colonel Redborn didn't think he just reacted. "I am going with you," he said resolutely.

Slightly stunned that he wanted to leave his team, Matrix spun on her heels to face the Colonel again. She had a pretty good idea why he wanted to follow her, but with time as an issue, she chose not to argue. "Keep up," she replied with a quirk of her mouth. The two separated from the group and Matrix briskly led the way back to the lift while the strike team hurried to assist their brethren.

Unknown to them, Major Baker had been watching and slipped from the shadows as the two groups went off their separate ways. Major Baker cautiously made his way over to where Dr. Jamison lay on the floor. "Sir, the self-destruct has been triggered. We have to get out," he softly whispered.

CHAPTER 11

Countdown to My Destruction

"They were not expecting anyone coming from below, but they likely have left guards by the elevator above us," Matrix said as she pressed the up arrow to call the lift's car.

Colonel Redborn nodded in understanding, and they both stepped through the opening doors. Once inside the car, Matrix pressed the button for the ground floor and the elevator began its climb. Both readied their weapons and prepared for the doors to open. For Colonel Redborn, that could not happen soon enough. The lift was slow, and the ride up was awkward. Matrix stood like a statue while the Colonel shifted restlessly from foot to foot making his boots squeak slightly. His eyes flitted over to Matrix a couple of times, but the girl never flinched. Finally, a soft ding signaled the doors were opening. Colonel Redborn breathed out a sigh of relief, and the two took aim. When the doors slid open both occupants of the car rushed out, but there was no one in sight.

"This way," Matrix indicated with the swing of her gun, then she quickly proceeded down the hall.

Colonel Redborn had not had much of an opportunity to see the inside of the base, but it was clear that the main level was in much better condition than anything else he had seen. He allowed his mind to wander slightly as Matrix hurriedly led him through the labyrinth of hallways to their destination. She was keeping him updated on where they were. It was obvious that she was trying to make him feel more comfortable and trust her, but he appreciated the effort and it helped fill the silence. He remembered that she said something about the base being renovated and added onto several times over the years, but when they reached a set of double doors that looked like they belonged to a psychiatric ward rather than a military base, he was a little unsure. He was studying what was obviously one of the updated additions when Matrix informed him that this was the part of the base where she and her team were kept. The Colonel only nodded in response but noticed how she struggled for the right word before settling for "kept." She had never been in a position where she had to explain why her team was on the base before, it was not something that Dr. Jamison had wanted advertised and those who visited were usually aware of their purpose.

Matrix scanned an identification card to gain access and a small green light lit at the corner of the door. Matrix pressed down on the handle and the door clicked open. The hall they entered was much newer than the rest of the base he had seen. The white walls only intensified the resemblance to a hospital, but the minimal lighting in this section of the base gave off a bluish glow that reflected off the pristine surfaces. On second thought, it reminded the Colonel of a futuristic lab, something out of a science fiction movie. Well, he supposed it was, and that thought only increased his concern about what kind of people he was dealing with. He didn't know anything about this girl, and he didn't like not having all of the information.

Matrix was obviously highly trained, and it did not escape his notice that she never allowed him to fully follow behind her. She carefully stayed half a step ahead of him. Far enough ahead to lead, but not far enough that she couldn't see the barrel of his weapon. And was this teammate she kept referencing a child too? As if on cue, the girl stopped and raised a hand to her earpiece.

"Blade are you still in the base?" Matrix asked a hint of concern lacing her words. There was no response. "Red Phoenix, please respond," she tried again, but there was still no response. She hoped that meant that he had moved out of range again but thought that he would have notified her.

"Did your friend get out?" Colonel Redborn asked in a tone Matrix was surprised she could not quite identify.

She considered the Colonel's question and tone for a moment, deciding how much she wanted to reveal and what his intentions were. "There was no reply," she said settling for the truth, but keeping all emotion out of her voice. "You should contact your men," Matrix suggested, deflecting the conversation away from Blade before the Colonel could ask any more questions. The Colonel locked eyes with Matrix seeming to decide if he wanted to split his focus on her but nodded and grabbed a radio from his belt.

Major Lockfire, Colonel Redborn's second in command for this mission, established radio contact with his commanding officer at 0707 hours, March twenty-second, 2003.

"Our forces have split their men, sir. We will overpower them soon," Major Lockfire yelled over the heavy gunfire echoing in the background and turned to begin firing again. *Superior officers always had a way of making contact at the worst time*, he thought as a series of bullets flew over his head.

"Very good, Major. You only have five minutes; will you make it through in time?" he heard Colonel Redborn's voice filter through the radio again.

"I'll do my best, sir," the Major dutifully responded before placing the radio back in its pocket. *Talking to you takes up more of that time*, the Major thought to himself. His thoughts were bordering on insubordinate, but he could not find it in himself to care when a stray bullet pierced the wall a few millimeters above his head. He was only stuck with this man for the remainder of the mission, Major Lockfire reminded himself for the umpteenth time since the operation had begun.

Having gathered all of the information he wanted, Colonel Redborn returned his radio to his belt and began turning to face where Matrix had been standing before he had turned his back for a relative measure of privacy to speak to his second in command. "My men have made progress, they should..." the Colonel stopped short when he saw that the girl he was speaking to was no longer standing behind him. "Darn girl teleports," he cursed under his breath as he moved to look for her.

There was only one way that she could have gone, so Colonel Redborn proceeded down the creepy hall in the creepy blue lighting. It was not that he was afraid, but in his opinion, a military base had no reason to look like a sci-fi loony bin. Seriously, who authorized this place? And he would also like to have a word with the interior designer. There was just something ever since he was assigned for the job that did not quite feel right. An assault on an American base, on American soil, mind control, an evil scientist, child soldiers, and a freakin' creepy hallway! This is not what he signed up for when he joined the military. Letting out a long, suffering sigh, he began his search.

The Colonel cautiously searched the hallways, checking each room he passed until he came to what looked like the access to some kind of prison cell block or where the dangerous patients would be kept. The wall was mostly made of thick glass with a door in the center. Beyond the wall was another short hallway with four solid white doors, each with a small, vertical, rectangle window slightly off to the side. As he got closer to the door, he saw that it was much like the previous door he and Matrix passed through to enter the creepy lab section of the base and that it had already been cracked open. "Creepy hallways and creepy doors," he muttered exasperatedly.

Colonel Redborn slowly and gently pushed the door open even though he could already see what was on the other side. The entire base was starting to give him a bad feeling and he was not willing to take any chances. The cool metal of the door sent a chill through his spine as his hand contacted with its metal frame, and a slight static shock caused him to jump in surprise, skyrocketing his already heightened nerves. The first door on the right was halfway open and a dim light was spilling into the hallway along with a slight rustling sound. The Colonel took a deep shuttering breath knowing he needed to go check the room, then laughed silently at himself. He was being ridiculously childish for a highly trained member of an elite strike force and he knew it. He was not even the child in this whole situation! That thought only served to initiate a round of hysterical laughter as he stumbled forward slightly breathless. He was shaking his head at himself and decided he needed to focus and stop being ridiculous. So, he summoned the needed courage by drawing from his pride, but just as he prepared to round the corner to look in the room, the girl he was looking for came rushing through the doorway with her weapon drawn.

"We need to leave, there is little time remaining," Matrix said to the stunned colonel, a hint of a smirk behind her serious exterior.

Colonel Redborn was still trying to regain his composure from the heart attack she just gave him. Seriously, she is lucky he didn't shoot her! On second thought, it might not be too late to shoot her now. "Colonel, it is imperative that we leave immediately," Matrix said again with a hint of irritation directed at the frozen colonel. Yeah, he was definitely going to shoot her.

After the Colonel had turned to speak with his second in command, Matrix had taken the opportunity to go and recover the laptop from her room. She told herself that it was the most efficient course of action and that she was saving time by not waiting so she could guide the Colonel through the base, and that she could pick him up on her way back. But, as she got closer to her team's rooms, she realized that she really just needed to be alone. Her entire life was inside these walls and the people on this base, but that was all going to be blown apart in less than five minutes. Of course, she would never admit it, but the thought of that terrified her. Had this all been a mistake? She had nowhere to go, no one to go to, and she didn't even know if Blade had made it out. She was a survivor; her entire team was made of survivors. They were the four that survived. She had the skills to make it anywhere she went, but in the past, she always had a purpose and a place to return to. Her entire fate had been dictated by Dr. Jamison since she entered the Phoenix program at the age of four.

And then there was Jamison... Dr. Jamison, she didn't even know what to call him anymore. She felt betrayed but also like she was betraying him. Her hand came up to the scanner by the door that would grant her access to her team's room. She had performed that very action countless times and the familiar motion managed to calm her slightly, if only for a moment. This was the last time that she would perform the simple action. Illogically, she found that she was sad to realize it. It was not that her life had been easy or enjoyable here, but Jamison had been right about one thing, they were special, and he did help them reach their full potential. She supposed in a way she owed him for that. She knew what other people were like and the children her age. She knew how to think like them, act like them, she knew how to become them. That was her job, infiltration, but that life was never going to be hers. She knew too much, had seen too much... had done too much. She could never truly be them.

Matrix furiously brushed back a rebellious tear as she

opened the door to her room. Secure the laptop and get out, that was the main priority right now. Matrix quickly opened the door to her room and rushed in to retrieve the laptop and its case. She quickly checked to make sure that none of the data had been tampered with, then closed it back up in the case. Before she left, Matrix glanced around her room. She did not really have any personal items. Jamison had never approved of that kind of thing, but there was one item, a small locket tucked safely in the corner of the bottom drawer of her dresser, with the letters V.E.L. engrave on the back. She had it with her when she was taken and had managed to keep it hidden for over a decade. Matrix hadn't looked at it in years. It was the last remnant she had of her former life. Without a second thought, Matrix retrieved the locket from the drawer and placed it around her neck. She took one last look around the room, grabbed one of her ready-packed bags, drew her weapon, and ran from the room.

Matrix was slightly stunned that she had not heard Colonel Redborn in the hall. She must have been deeper in her thoughts than she realized. It was a careless mistake, but a confident mask quickly fell into place to hide her surprise, and she advised him that they should leave as quickly as possible. When he remained unresponsive, she briefly thought that she may have to drag him out, but slowly the Colonel nodded in compliance. The action also serving to clear his head. Matrix looked the Colonel in the eye and nodded back when she was certain she had his full attention. "Quickly, there is a side exit only a short distance from here. We have under two minutes remaining," she said motioning for him to follow as she sprinted down the hall and to the right.

With only two minutes remaining to make it a safe distance away from the base, Matrix ran as quickly as she could, only occasionally glancing behind her to make sure Colonel Redborn was still there. Matrix did a quick calculation in her head as she ran. They were already on the far end of the building since it was added onto the original portion of the base, and the right-side exit was only thirty seconds away at their current pace. After they exited the building there would be one minute and thirty seconds remaining. There was no way for her to determine how much explosives Dr. Jamison had used, but by her calculations, there should be plenty of time for them to reach a safe distance.

The base was in a slight valley and surrounded on all sides by a dense forest. The uphill slope from the right side of the base was the steepest of the four sides and the tree line was roughly two hundred yards from the base. When the pair reached the doors, Matrix only slowed enough to prevent herself from slamming into the door before positioning her hands to intersect the crash bar. As the door opened Matrix rushed through, with Colonel Reborn right behind her to slip through the closing door.

Matrix's mind was flooded with thoughts and doubts as she ran up the hill to the relative safety of the forest. Thoughts such as the fate of Corbet and Ivy, they had been victims of Jamison just like her, did the strike force make it out, and what could have happened to Blade. As soon as she reached the trees, Matrix stopped and turned to face the base. She was panting and out of breath from the adrenaline-fueled sprint, but her mind was on full alert as she stared at the base with wide eyes. She tried desperately one last time to contact Blade from the outside of the base, but her hand fell to her side as her pleas were met with silence. The base, her home, exploded into great pillars of flames only moments later. The force of the explosion swept through her like a tidal wave, and she was forced to hold onto the thin trees serving as her cover to maintain balance. The sound echoed through the trees, and smoke billowed from the flames that were leaping from every corner of the destruction. The sky above was painted brilliant shades of red and gold as the sun was cresting the horizon, giving it the appearance that it was burning with the base. A bloody sky to follow a bloody night.

Matrix stood in awe of the sight before her, unable to draw her eyes away, unable to think. Even from the tree line, ash and debris hung in the air making it harder to catch her breath. She was numb. She didn't know if she should cry, celebrate, or scream, but right now she couldn't feel any of those things. She could feel that her hands were shaking, but it was no use trying to still them. It seemed that they were not going to listen to her today, so she shoved them in her pockets and her attention was drawn back to the field of rubble in front of her. The explosion had been even bigger than she had expected. Jamison must have had the entire base rigged with explosives, maybe even tied into the electrical systems or boiler room. There would be no traces of his unethical operations, and there was no way anyone could have survived.

A muffled cough behind her caused the young special operative to whip around due to the adrenaline still coursing through her system. She had seen Colonel Redborn move farther back into the trees when they first arrived, but her attention had been drawn elsewhere. His hand still held the radio he had likely just used to contact his team, and he was looking at her with something resembling sympathy. Matrix wanted to say something to deflect the attention away from herself, but her tongue seemed to have gone silent. "Did your men make it out?" Matrix forced out, trying but failing to keep her voice steady.

"They did," he replied in a soft voice. It was much different than the side of the Colonel Matrix had seen up until this point. It was much softer, gentler, like he was trying to soothe a small child. She was not a child. Her childhood had been stolen from her just as it was beginning. Matrix had noticed a wedding band on the Colonel's left hand and wondered if he happened to have done this before. Or was he playing her? Maybe he wanted to use her the way Jamison had! Matrix jerked slightly at that thought and subconsciously began backing away, her eyes moving to his hands.

The Colonel, sensing her panic, tracked her eyes and raised his hand in a pacifying gesture, showing her that they were now empty. "Easy, it's ok," he said keeping his voice low and even. From what he was able to deduce, this girl was highly trained, dangerous, scared, and had just lost everything she knew. Not a great combination. Other than that, he really did not know anything about her, but he knew he needed to tread very lightly. He knew he probably should not mention Dr. Jamison or the base and definitely not her teammate, but what did that leave? Colonel Redborn took a deep breath, just get her talking he decided. "You know, you can call me Mike if you would like," he said thinking that maybe a first name could establish some trust. No response, and she looked like she was searching for the best escape route to bolt. Ok, this might be difficult, but he was not ready to give up yet. "Is Matrix your real name?" he tried, hoping a direct question might yield better results. Matrix's eyes instantly snapped up to meet his, but the Colonel couldn't quite read her. Ok, definitely a strong response, but he wasn't sure if that was good or bad.

Matrix held his eyes for several seconds and just when he thought he wasn't going to get any farther with that line of questioning, she surprised him. "Varian," Matrix whispered hesitantly. It felt strange, wrong but almost right, it was the first time she could remember saying the name.

She had said it so softly the Colonel was almost unsure that she had actually spoken. "Varian?" he tentatively asked, eliciting a small nod from the girl. "Varian, can you tell me how long you have been here?" he asked. The Colonel was afraid he was pushing his luck, but still, the girl began to answer.

"Ten years, three months, fourteen days," she answered almost robotically.

Colonel Redborn inhaled deeply, this girl had spent most of her life under the control of, from what he could tell, was a mad man. He really had no idea what he was dealing with, and certainly was not trained for this kind of thing. Perhaps it would be best if he could just get her to someone who knows how to deal with this kind of thing, but to get her to follow him, he was pretty sure he would need to build some trust first.

The two were at a standoff. The Colonel had no idea what to say and Matrix certainly was not helping him. Unless staring blankly into his soul could be considered helping.

This girl just lost everything, how was he supposed to approach her? But then he remembered he was dealing with a child. She may not act like one, but she couldn't be much older than his own daughter. "I'm sorry about your home," not that he could ever consider the cell he saw to be a home for a child, but to her, it must have been home. Matrix bit her lower lip slightly, and the Colonel smiled sadly. His daughter always did that when she was about to cry, but this girl seemed a lot more disciplined and unlikely to wear her emotions so openly. But still, it stirred something inside him that had him wanting to embrace the child. "I have a daughter," the Colonel said pausing for a moment, "She's probably not much younger than you."

That caught Matrix's attention, why would he give her personal information like that? It is never a good idea to reveal unnecessary information in the field. Unless he was still trying to manipulate her, but something told her that was not the case. Matrix swallowed thickly, "I don't know my father."

As a father himself, that was heartbreaking to hear. He would do anything for his little girl, Violet Sage Redborn. Working on an elite, military strike force, he was not able to be around as much as he would have liked, and he missed her every day. But, he told himself that he was making the world a safer place for his little girl. "Do you have any family you can go to?" the Colonel asked. From what he had seen, he highly doubted it, but still felt that he should ask.

Matrix looked back over her shoulder at the still-burning rubble of the collapsed base, then looked back to Colonel Redborn and shook her head. She had not had a family since she was four. And that family she was forced to forget. She was a tool now, a weapon, a project, one of Dr. Jamison's greatest experiments. That is what the Phoenix team represented. Their past lives were gone. They had a new life now, but it was not like their old lives.

The Colonel was unsure what to say to that, and the one thought that continued to run through his mind was that he really was not the person for this, but she seemed to be relaxing a little. He really hoped he wasn't pushing his luck again, but he couldn't just leave her here. "My team works for the United States government, would you like to come with us?" he asked gently, trying to not push her. But, as soon as the words left his mouth, he realized that it was a mistake.

"No!" The young girl's eyes went wide again, followed by several fast steps back, before finally, she ran.

Just like that, all of his work and any trust he had built was lost. What was he thinking! The girl had spent ten years of her life held in a United States military base. Or at least it looked like a United States military base. But of course, that was going to scare her off. Colonel Redborn stood staring at the trees where Matrix had disappeared shaking his head. There was no way he would be able to find her in the dense foliage and chasing her was likely to result in her becoming more afraid of him and him getting shot. Crap.

CHAPTER 12

We Are with You Colonel

After Matrix ran off, Colonel Redborn decided there was nothing left to do but rejoin his team. He doubted that there would be anything worth recovering from the destruction of the base, but that wasn't his area anyway. He would report back to his superiors and leave that mess to be sorted out by whatever casualty enjoyed sifting through destruction. With that thought, he turned to walk away. "Time to return home," he spoke softly to himself. But, as soon as the words were out of his mouth, the Colonel froze mid-step and dropped his head. Slowly, Colonel Redborn turned back to face the debris again. There had to be countless men buried under that rubble, many of them his own men. Men who counted on him to lead them not only to victory but also back home. Suddenly he found a new respect for those "casualties" as he called them. He had forgotten that not only do they recover cool toys in this kind of situation, but they make sure everyone goes home. Truthfully, he hated being the ranking officer. It was his responsibility to make sure everyone got home, but how many had he failed today? "Too many," he sighed, "It's always too many." Shaking his head somberly, the Colonel resumed his path to meet up with his remaining team.

The majority of the strike force had evacuated the base through the front, and those who had not were already joining them. Colonel Redborn was bringing up the rear and the last to join the gathering group. Colonel Redborn walked straight through the middle of the group not bothering to look any of his men in the face. Had he looked up, a few of the men wore expressions of sympathy, a few openly showed their anger, but most simply maintained a professional front.

The strike force looked expectantly at their commanding officer as he continued walking until his back was facing the team. Several steps separated the Colonel from the group before he stopped. "Let's go home," he said in a low, tired voice before continuing on his path. He inclined his head slightly behind him but didn't bother to turn around to see if his team was following.

The large military transport aircraft that had delivered the team was waiting nearly a mile hike away in the closest clearing able to accommodate its size. The Colonel was busy forcing himself not to count how many men were returning to the plane when Lieutenant Carson came up beside him.

The young Lieutenant looked at him with caring eyes, but the Colonel could not bring himself to face her, not yet. "You did your best, sir. The mission was a success," the brave

Lieutenant futilely tried to convince Colonel Redborn.

At first, the Colonel ignored her attempts to comfort him but eventually he crumbled. "I lost a third of my men, Lieutenant. I'm sorry if I can't see how that is a success," he ground out. At first, his voice was low enough that the others couldn't hear him, but by the second sentence, his tone had grown cold and hostile. He knew it wasn't fair to Lieutenant Carson, but she was still too young, too naive to understand the burdens of command. It was his responsibility as their commanding officer to make sure everyone got home.

At first instinct, Lieutenant Carson wanted to feel hurt, but she knew that his anger was not directed at her. "They were ready for us, sir. There was nothing more you could have done," she tried again, but when her words were met with silence, eventually she too fell back with the rest of the strike force. Leaving the melancholy colonel somberly marching ahead with his remaining team following behind.

The flight home had been filled with a heavy silence that no one seemed willing to break. Only occasional low whispers drowned out by the roar of the engines managed to pierce a hole in the absence of chatter. For some, the two-hour flight seemed to drag on for ages. For Colonel Redborn, time passed as though he were floating in a heavy fog. His eyes were glued to the floor in front of him and his back was rigid, but his mind drifted just on the edge of consciousness. The Colonel barely noticed when the plane landed, only being broken out of his trance by his men filing out the plane. Even then, he numbly walked from the plane with his head miles away.

Upon their arrival, members of the team were selected to report for a debriefing. Colonel Redborn slowly trudged into the conference room, this was one debrief he was not looking forward to.

"Gentlemen, please take a seat," a slightly gruff voice instructed.

Strange, the Colonel thought, he knew that voice from somewhere. Reluctantly, the Colonel pried his eyes from their downcast position on the floor to be level with the man whose voice he heard. When Colonel Redborn found the man who had spoken, he nearly froze in shock.

"Good morning Colonel, would you care to take a seat," the Secretary of Defense asked in a well-practiced, polite, formal tone.

"Yes, sir," the Colonel managed to force out, responding to the inquiry more like a command. Just when he thought his day could not get any worse, the Secretary of Defense decided to sit in on the worst debriefing of his life.

Upon hearing about the strike force's return, the Secretary of Defense boarded a private jet to rush to the base. *They weren't supposed to return, what could have gone wrong?* the Secretary thought in frustration as he marched to the conference room to attend the strike team's debriefing. Men in the halls jumped to solute the high ranking official as he passed, but the Secretary of Defense was too concerned with matters of his own to spare them much more than a fleeting glance. He politely acknowledged the other men in the conference room as he entered, then he sat in the closest chair to wait for the team's arrival. Any attempt to ask why the Secretary of Defense was attending the debriefing in person were instantly shot down by a withering, passive-aggressive expression of someone who clearly did not want to be questioned.

As everyone settled into their seats, the Secretary of Defense began asking his questions. "So, Colonel Redborn, you led the strike force on the base. Is that correct?" he began.

The Colonel, obviously struggling not to fidget, was instantly thrust back into mulling over the events of the last twenty-four hours. No longer distracted by the surprise of being debriefed by the Secretary of Defense, the Colonel was now slipping back into the headspace he had remained in throughout the return flight. "Yes, sir," he responded for the second time since entering the conference room, but with less enthusiasm than the first time. He knew it would not be the last time he uttered the phrase today.

It was one of the Colonel's superiors to speak next. The military man sat with his shoulders square exuding the confidence of an officer. His light brown hair was flecked with gray and the lines around his eyes spoke of years in a stressful position. All of this gave him the appearance of someone much older and hardened, but his warm brown eyes, while serious, seemed sympathetic toward the Colonel. "Was the operation a success, Colonel?" General McKendry asked. The General's eyes carefully studied Colonel Redborn as he considered his answer carefully.

Seeming to have made up his mind, he simply answered, "The base was destroyed, Sir."

General McKendry nodded in understanding and looked to the others present for questions. He knew that they would go deeper as the debriefing continued. It was still surprising to the General that Colonel Redborn had been put in charge of the strike force in the first place. The Colonel was a good man, but he did not have the experience necessary to lead an operation of the magnitude this one had been. Yet, that someone further up the chain of command had specifically requested him, left the General somewhat perplexed.

The Colonel was asked to give a full report of everything that transpired up until the point that the team returned. Dutifully, Colonel Redborn began to recount the events that occurred, beginning with their arrival at the base.

The four men, including himself, that were asked to attend the debriefing included the Colonel and the men that led the other three groups that divided up to overtake the base. He starts by telling about his team setting up in the tree line, but his voice falters as he begins to tell about the first wave or men sent into the base. The Colonel collects himself with a deep breath and resumes his report with a certain level of detachment from his words. His near robotic voice filled the room, only pausing when a question was asked. This continued for some time, however, when he reaches the point where Matrix proposed an alliance with the strike force, there was a sudden increase in questions. Who is Matrix? What did she want? Why was she there? And where is she now?

At first, Colonel Reborn attempted to keep up with all of the questions directed to him, but eventually, running on little sleep and with the last bit of adrenaline draining from his system, it was becoming increasingly harder to focus his thoughts. He really just wanted to finish his report and find the closest shower. Did he stink? He probably stinks, he decided. Casually he began subtlety shifting to see if he did indeed stink when he was abruptly pulled out of his thoughts.

"Colonel... Colonel, Colonel!" Colonel Redborn's attention was brought back to the meeting by the rather angry-sounding voice of the Secretary of Defense. The strong, deep voice of the Secretary was startling enough to bring the Colonel's mind back to the present, but the eyes that met his when he "rejoined" the meeting left him wishing he hadn't. Up until this point, the Secretary of Defense has seemed content to observe the debriefing for the most part, but now it appeared he had questions of his own personal interest.

"Colonel Redborn, you said that this "Matrix" worked for Dr. Jamison, the head scientist on the base, and that Dr. Jamison is the one who converted or "brainwashed" your men, as I believe you put it. Is this correct?" the Secretary asked with a slightly condescending undertone in his voice.

The Colonel swallowed hard before answering, "That is correct, sir."

"What can you tell me about the doctor?" the Secretary of Defense asked, seeming to move away from the line questioning about the girl.

"Not very much, sir. There wasn't time for questions," the Colonel answered, for the moment happy that he was no longer having to answer why he had trusted Matrix. But that feeling quickly faded as the Secretary continued to ask about Dr. Jamison. All of the Secretary's questions began to point to one thing; *Where is Dr. Jamison?* None of the other three strike team members that were in the debriefing room had been with him when he had beaten the doctor, but the mention of Dr. Jamison's name was beginning to make him very uncomfortable. He knew what he did was wrong, but the man was a monster, and the things he did to his men and those children were unspeakable. Colonel Redborn told the Secretary what he saw when he entered Dr. Jamison's laboratory and the things he had done to his men. And finally, what he himself had done to Dr. Jamison.

The expression on the Secretary's face was one of pure outrage, with no attempt to hide it. But it was rivaled only by the expression on Colonel Redborn's. He knew the name of every man Dr. Jamison had taken from him. As their faces flashed through his mind, the Colonel stared into the Secretary's eyes. "There was nothing more I could have done, sir," the Colonel says, remembering the words of Lieutenant Carson, "There was nothing left of them to save." The Colonel's voice trails off and his gaze falls to where his hands rest folded in his lap. He says this trying to convince himself more than the others present in the conference room. He could have at least tried to save them he thinks, now fighting the burning sensation in his eyes again. When he looks back up, the Secretary of Defense is still staring at him, the fiery rage burning intensely in his eyes. Colonel Redborn half expects his court-martial to be held in that room. And maybe he deserves it.

"How could you have done that?" the Secretary asks, his voice taking on an almost distraught ache.

Leaving those men behind, it was unspeakable Colonel Redorn thought noticing how the Secretary could not even say the words. "They were gone, sir, and there was no time. The enemy was closing in, and I had the rest of my men to think about," he says solemnly, trying to explain himself, though it is just as painful for him. Truthfully, in that moment, if Matrix had not been there, he might have gotten the rest of his team killed by not taking charge of the situation when one of his men had discharged his weapon and given away their position.

"Colonel, you killed the doctor in cold blood," the Secretary of Defense spat out.

Colonel Redborn was shocked by the nature of the accusation for a moment. There was a lot left unspoken in what the Secretary said but clearly insinuated by his remark. What he did was wrong, and he knew it, but was that really what the Secretary of Defense was angry about? At the end of the day, Colonel Redborn was not going to lose any sleep over the loss of Dr. Jamison. He was a cruel, evil man. Maybe, under different circumstances, and if he had been thinking clearer, the Colonel would have taken him prisoner, but still, not one person in their right mind could say that the world was not a better place without him in it. With the Secretary still glaring daggers into his very soul, the Colonel was unable to contain his opinion anymore. "He killed my men, sir," Colonel Redborn began raising his voice, "I take full responsibility for my actions, but twenty-four of the seventy men that I left with are never going home thanks to him. I will not be mourning his loss."

Sensing the escalation in the argument, General McKendry decided it was time to step in. "Colonel Redborn, you are out of line," he reprimanded, rising to his feet. "I believe that is enough for today. I expect everything to be in your report, Colonel," the general commanded, placing additional stress on the word *everything*. He was attempting to subtly let the colonel off the hook for the rest of the day without making it too obvious.

The Colonel would have to be disciplined for his actions, but something was not adding up in General McKendry's eyes. Concluding the debriefing for the day would allow him the time necessary to investigate. General McKendry had known the Secretary of Defense for years. They were never close, but when you serve with someone, you get to know them. He almost seemed angry that the mission had been a success, indifferent about the men lost, but distraught that Dr. Jamison had been killed. It was all enough to make him suspicious, but he wasn't sure exactly what he was suspicious of yet. The General recalled hearing that he had been held captive a while back but knew he would have been cleared by a psychologist since then. Sighing, General McKendry followed the men filing out of the conference room.

As soon as General McKendry dismissed him, Colonel Redborn did not hesitate to storm out of the room, still feeling the Secretary glaring daggers into the back of his retrieving form.

The other three men from the strike force followed behind their commanding officer. The three exchanged a series of looks, nodding in agreement. Once the four of them were out of hearing range, one of the men began trying to speak to the Colonel. "Colonel, we all support your position," he began, glancing at the other two and receiving two nods in response. "What that man did to Jackson and her team..." he continued, "He deserved everything he got, Sir." The emotion was tangible in his voice. He had been friends with Jackson before the mission and felt that he would likely have done the same in the Colonel's position.

"I appreciate that, but I want all of you to stay out of this," Colonel Redborn stressed, stopping and turning to face his three men, "None of you need to get involved in this."

"Sir, we are all involved in this," they said in agreement.

"You saw that they were ready for us the second we arrived," one of the other team leaders spoke up, "There was no way we were supposed to get out of there at all."

"At the end of the day, we all know what we signed up for, Sir," the last man added in.

The Colonel looked between each of his men with an assessing gaze. None of them wavered and the Colonel allowed himself to relax slightly. He respected every member of his team, and it was nice to know that they had his back too. "Thank you, all of you," the Colonel nodded with a hint of a genuine smile.

The Colonel was just about to go and find that shower when something caught his attention.

"Lieutenant?" he called to the man who had already begun walking away.

"Yes, Sir?" the Lieutenant turned with an expectant look.

Colonel Redborn recognized the Lieutenant as one of the men from Major Lockfire's squad. "Where is Major Lockfire? He should have been at the debriefing," the Colonel asked in confusion.

"Oh, he asked me to fill in for him. I was the next highest ranking under him, Sir," the Lieutenant responded after taking a second to realize what Colonel Redborn was asking. He had said it as though that simple explanation would explain everything, but it was not common practice for a subordinate to simply fill in for a superior.

"Why did the Major ask you to fill in for him?" the Colonel asked taking on a slightly more serious tone.

"He said he was heading to medical," the Lieutenant explained, "He looked pretty exhausted, so I didn't argue with him, Sir."

Colonel Redborn nodded accepting the explanation. He was too tired himself to question the Lieutenant any further. His brain wasn't functioning anymore.

"Anything else, Sir," the Lieutenant asked.

He was beginning to sound a little too chipper to the Colonel's ears after the long mission. "No, that's all. Go get some rest Lieutenant," he said waving him off.

The Lieutenant smiled slightly at the Colonel and relaxed his shoulders resuming his path, but called over his should in a playful tone, "You too Colonel. You look like you need it."

Those young ones never seem to get tired, the Colonel muttered under his breath, but he let the poking slide in favor of showering. Yeah, he definitely did stink.

CHAPTER 13

One Shot Fired

Well, it turned out some of those casualties were not actually dead. In a small, dark holding cell, Major Lockfire paced back and forth in front of one of three young teens. There wasn't much room to pace in the cramped space, four steps to the left, turn, four steps to the right, turn, repeat. His two men that had accompanied him on the mission with the strike force stood guard at the door as unwavering as gargoyles. Major Lockfire released a deep breath, it was just a waiting game at this point. Waiting for the three to awaken from their drug-induced slumber.

His associates had performed their jobs expertly, breaking away from their respective teams and locating the Phoenixes. The first two had been easy, it appeared that they had already been rendered unconscious for them. The last, the oldest boy, had merely been a stroke of luck. Lockfire had been on his way out with his team when he spotted the boy near the tree line only a few hundred yards away. In the chaos of all the teams fleeing the building at the threat of its impending destruction, it was an easy feat to slip away unnoticed. One well-placed shot from a distance as the base exploded into fire and commotion, and his shot would be concealed. Then, quickly inject him with the same sedative concoction his associates would be giving the others, radio them the boy's location for pick up, and meet back up with his team before anyone can question his absence. It went perfectly.

Major Lockfire waved to get the attention of one of his men outside of the cell. The tall man that acknowledged him looked like a bodybuilder, but his strength was earned outside of a gym. The burly hand scanned a keycard on the glass door, and it cracked opened to allow the Major out. The second Major Lockfire turned his back, a dark shadow collided with his ribs. Blade wrestled a pen from the Major's pocket and charged the guard. However, before he had the chance to attack the larger man, the second guard thrust his taser into Blade's side. The boy's knees buckled, and he fell to the ground with a grunt of pain.

"I thought you Phoenixes were supposed to be tougher than that," the Major quipped with a chuckle.

"Well Major, that was where you shot him earlier," the guard holding the taser laughed out, a cruel smile twisting his face. Even from the ground, Blade glared at the man through his brow.

"Put him back in his cell," the Major ordered, still chuckling as he motioned with his hand. Blade didn't resist, but he didn't exactly help either as the guard half dragged him back into the cell. As the guard secured him to the chair, his eyes remained focused forward, a look of animosity securely in place. Once the guard finished roughly putting the cuffs into place, he gave Blade a cruel smile and exited the cell.

"What were you planning on doing with that pen anyway?" the guard asked humorously.

"You would be surprised what I have done with a pen," Blade answered darkly, his eyes never moving away from the Major on the other side of the glass.

Somehow, the tone of the boy's voice had the guard subconsciously taking a step back. The man didn't waste any more time before exiting the cell. Blade's eyes momentarily flicked over to the guard as the door sealed shut, before returning to bore into the face of his captor.

"Now someone's not in a very good mood," Major Lockfire teased with a cheeky smile as he came to stand in front of the glass. The teen's expression did not waver at the Major's mocking but remained persistent. Deprived of the reaction he was hoping, Major Lockfire sighed longingly and turned to move to the middle of the three cells. "Alright Phoenixes, you can quit playing possum now," he called out, but only with mock annoyance in his voice. A priceless look of utter confusion swept across Blade's face breaking through and mixing the pain and anger.

Major Lockfire sighed again dropping his head. "It's a metaphor," he mumbled. "Oh, I know you're all awake. You can stop pretending now," he elaborated seeing Blade's continued confusion. Slowly, the other two children in the room began to raise their heads. Their expressions closely mirroring their team leader. "Now, there we are," Major Lockfire said sweetly encouraging, "Now that we are all listening, I believe we have one missing."

CHAPTER 14

Damsel in de Press

The leaves caught in her hair, and the branches clawed into her arms. She could still feel the ghost of the heat from the explosion on her face mixing with the cool morning air. Rays of sunlight pierced the thick tree cover lighting her path, but she had no idea where she was going.

She could feel her heart pounding in her chest to the rhythm of her feet on the ground. She couldn't stop. She had to get away, but she had nowhere to go, and she had just lost the only person she trusted. She felt tears stream down her face for the first time in years as she skidded to a stop.

Matrix looked around, there were trees in every direction as far as she could see. She turned quickly scanning her surroundings, but it appeared that no one had followed her. The only thing she could hear were the sounds of her ragged breathing and the occasional chirp of a songbird awakening for another normal day. But this was not a normal day for Matrix.

What have I done? was the mantra that raced through her head before making it out into the world as she frantically mumbled the phrase. Slowly, the young girl sank down against the base of a large, old oak tree. She drew her knees into her chest and buried her head in her arms. This was all a mistake. What had she done?

She listened to every sound echoing through the forest and mixing with the murmur of her sobs. Small animals and wind gusting softly through the trees, shaking branches in every direction. It was too much. Too many sounds. Her mind was tracking each one of them, waiting for the one that was a threat. A strong gust of wind lifted her hair and cooled the tear tracks on her face when she looked up. A large limb behind her creaked under the force of the wind, that was all it took to push her over the edge. The world froze and everything seemed impossibly quiet in the wake of the sound. Matrix ran.

She didn't know how far she ran before she found the first sign of civilization. It was a small but fairly modern town in rural Nebraska. There was a gas station off by itself, a row of shops, a bakery, a diner, and a small café at the end of the shops.

Matrix knew that even if no one followed her, there would be people sent to the areas surrounding the base to find her. It was already nearing four o'clock and knowing that there would be someone looking for her, she knew she needed to act quickly.

Matrix visually scanned the town from the cover of the tree line. There were people going in and out of the businesses, busy with their daily lives. It wouldn't be difficult to blend in, Matrix concluded. Glancing down at her tattered uniform, she revised her previous conclusion. It will be easy to blend in once she acquires the proper attire. First on the list of what to do once you escape from a government lab and spend hours running through a dense forest; find a change of clothes.

Before moving into the town, she decided it would be best to make herself as inconspicuous as possible. First, she removed the black, tactical vest laden with gear, next, the black fingerless gloves she used for additional grip, her sidearm, other tools, and holsters from her belt, and finally the patches from her sleeves. Matrix looked down at herself for anything else that could be removed. The black cargo pants, black combat boots, and long-sleeved black crew neck weren't suspicious on their own, but together, along with their state of dirtied disarray, they were still likely to draw some attention. Promptly, she remembered the bag she had grabbed on her way out of the base. Its contents did not offer much, but it would be enough to last until she could find what she needed. Jamison had never allowed them to have very much available at one time, likely for fear that they would disappear, but the bags were designed to make for quick departure when a time-sensitive mission was assigned. Dr. Jamison kept all identification and currency to be given out just before the mission, but right now, Matrix was most interested in the jeans and black t-shirt tucked inside.

After changing, she carefully arranged as much of her gear to fit inside of the bag as possible, eliminating anything she did not need. In addition to the gear, Matrix also removed the laptop from its case and slipped it into the bag where it was likely to draw less attention. It was important not to leave any clues that she had been here, so she buried her vest and the other items that would not fit in her bag under the debris at the base of a large bush.

As a last step, Matrix removed the hair tie from her ponytail and smoothed the hair back before returning it to its previous position. There wasn't much she could do about the scratches from the trees or the bruises forming from the fights, but she did her best to cover anything she could and hoped that the rest would go unquestioned.

Matrix headed for the small but brightly colored café near the edge of the town for a safe place to take a look at the files stored on her laptop.

A small bell rang as she pushed open the glass door at the front of the shop, and Matrix internally cringed at the attention it drew. An overly cheerful barista greeted her as she entered, and Matrix slipped into character. "Good afternoon," Matrix replied back.

"What can I get you today, miss?" the barista questioned with a large smile still spread across her face.

At first, Matrix was not sure what to say. She had rarely been in this type of interaction on assignments but calmed herself and glanced at the menu over the barista's head, controlling her movement to appear as though it were a comfortably familiar task. "A green tea and a croissant, please," Matrix requested, matching the barista's cheerful tone. Matrix watched as the girl quickly tapped in her order.

"That will be four dollars and twenty-three cents," the barista said finishing entering the items.

Matrix reached into her pocket, pulling out the wallet that she liberated from one of two women arguing on the street corner at the entrance to the town. It had been unnaturally easy considering the two were quite involved in the heated argument. Matrix had casually bumped into one of the women, pocketing the wallet with ease. The obnoxious women had briefly turned to spit obscenities in her direction before once again becoming enthralled in her dispute. Matrix thought back with a professional fondness for the interaction as she counted out the change.

The barista took the money gratefully but hesitated as she saw the cuts marring the skin on Matrix's outstretched arm. However, she recovered quickly with a soft, nervous laugh and deposited the money into the register. "Can I get a name for your order?" she asked, her voice slightly less cheerful than before.

As the words left the barista's mouth, Matrix froze. She had never had to give her name to a civilian. On assignment, she had always been given an alias or cover story, but this wasn't a mission and there wasn't someone she was pretending to be. Before she could fully register what she was saying, the name was falling out of her mouth.

"Varian." "Varian, that's a pretty name. Your order will be ready in a few minutes," the barista said sweetly.

Matrix nodded her thanks, not really sure what to do next. There were very few customers scattered about in the café at the odd hour. Most were patrons of the small town who had stopped in to chat. Matrix spotted a vacant, two-person table in the far corner near a back exit that offered a clear view of the window. Casually, she made her way over and took a seat with her back to the wall. She took a moment to scan the inside of the café before shifting her attention to check outside the window. With no one catching her eye,

Matrix took a deep breath and settled into her chair. It was nice to be comfortable inside for a while, but she was not deluded enough to believe that she was actually safe here. She would take a moment to rest, then would be on her way again.

"Varian," the barista called out.

It felt strange to hear her name used in that way, and she hesitated to look around the café before going up to retrieve her order. The hot tea was in a white paper cup, and the croissant was placed on a napkin. Matrix took the items in each hand and offered the barista a grateful smile before returning to her seat.

Once back at the table, Matrix took a bite of her croissant before setting both it and the drink on the table. She then slipped the bag from her shoulder and set it on the floor by her chair. So far, no one was paying any attention to her, but she had a feeling that pulling out the laptop was going to attract more attention than she had hoped. Matrix leaned over to feel the contents of her bag. After running her fingers across the smooth edge of the laptop, she switched her attention to feeling for the device she had secured from Jamison's lab, also known as Project Marionette. Feeling the reassuring grooves on the surface of the metal, she was satisfied the device was safe for now. Matrix had no way of knowing if anyone would be looking for the device. From what she was able to gather, Jamison had been working the project alone, and from what she saw of the file, it was not his first time working with the device. Matrix withdrew her hand from the bag, opting to wrap the shoulder strap around her ankle for added security, before returning to the task of her food.

Matrix drinks the last of her tea in one long sip and

crumples the napkin from her croissant. She had been in one spot for long enough and it was time to start moving before anyone became interested in her. She quickly checked her things and prepared to make her exit.

Too late, Matrix thought as she saw a middle-aged lady approaching, with two children following close behind her. As the lady neared the table, Matrix stood throwing her bag over one shoulder, hoping she could evade any interaction. However, before Matrix could make her escape, the woman had come to stand directly in her path.

"Hello dear, I don't recognize you from around here. I'm Mrs. Doles, what's your name?" the lady asked Matrix with a smile.

Matrix hesitated again at the request for her name. This woman didn't seem to be a threat, but it would be impossible to be too cautious in her present situation. Slowly, she slipped into character, ready to do whatever was necessary to maintain her cover. "My name is Varian," she answered with a light tone, pausing as she manufactured the rest of her cover story. "And I'm not from here. My family and I are just passing through," she continued, still keeping her tone light and friendly, but the way the lady was looking at her was beginning to make her uncomfortable. Her instincts were screaming that she needed to get out of there as quickly as possible. Before this lady could ask too many questions.

"Oh, I understand. Where are your parents now, honey?" Mrs. Doles asked.

Matrix had a fairly good idea of where this was going, seeing how the lady was running an assessing gaze over the various cuts and bruises on her face and arms in much the same way that the barista had. However, with no obvious out, Matrix decided to stay in character as long as possible, in an attempt to talk her way out of the predicament. Her story only needed to last long enough for her to get outside and disappear, so it didn't need to be perfect, just consistent she decided. "They took our car to get a flat tire changed. We hit something in the road a couple miles back, and this was the closest place with a repair shop we could find," Matrix explained, "They let me come in here to get a snack while the car is being worked on."

The lady nodded in response, still seeming to assess the story.

Mrs. Doles had entered the café with her two boys intending to grab a coffee before heading home for the day. She walked up to the barista, offering a friendly greeting before placing her order. While waiting for her coffee to be prepared, she had noticed the young girl sitting in the corner with a bag by her feet. In the small-town café, people got to know each other. Mrs. Doles could name all of the regulars sitting in their usual seats but couldn't place the girl. Upon taking a closer look at the young girl, she noticed the fresh cuts and bruises that littered the girl's skin. There were some obvious signs that she had attempted to cover some of the damage but had not been very successful. Her first thoughts went to the girl being a runaway, and just with the amount of damage she could see, it looked like she had a good reason. Being a mother herself, it was impossible for her to ignore the girl. If there was something she could do, she needed to do it.

Now, listening to the girl explain why she was there, Mrs. Doles was almost tempted to believe her. But, experiences of her own led her to make an effort to dig deeper. In her mind, the kind lady believed she was helping, and it was touching to see someone care. But Matrix needed to find a way out before Mrs. Doles could bring any more unwanted attention down on her. With nothing better to do, some of the patrons were already beginning to watch the interaction. Matrix shifted uncomfortably under the eyes on her, but if the lady noticed her discomfort, there was no outward sign.

After Matrix explained that her parents were at the repair shop, Mrs. Doles decided that she would like to talk with them and if everything seemed fine, she would drop the matter.

"Oh, I'm sorry to hear about your car. I was actually just heading home with my boys. Since it looks like you've finished up, I would be happy to walk you to the shop," Mrs. Doles tried to offer casually.

"I appreciate the offer, but I'll be fine," Matrix protested and tried to sidestep the lady. However, with the two children at her sides, there was not enough room in the small café.

"It's no trouble at all. I insist," Mrs. Doles continued to press.

Matrix was desperate to find a way out but was continually blocked by the lady. There could be someone looking for her any second.

"Please, I don't know you," Matrix tried switching tactics and letting a note of fear slip into her voice. At first, the approach seemed to have the desired effect. Mrs. Doles took a step back from where she had gotten imposingly close to the girl. It was best not to appear threatening to the girl, but she was trying to hold her there.

"It's alright, dear. I want to help you," the lady said, gesturing to the marks on her arms.

It seemed Mrs. Doles was taking a different approach as well, a more direct approach.

"I don't need your help," Matrix proclaimed in frustration, but still not slipping out of character.

Mrs. Doles offered her a sad but mistakenly understanding look. "I know you don't, dear, but I can help you," she said sincerely, "I've been where you are. I can take you somewhere safe where they can't hurt you."

Even though Matrix knew that the lady was misreading the situation, her offer did sound tempting. She didn't have anywhere to go, and this lady seemed to genuinely want to help her. Matrix was just about to take Mrs. Doles up on her offer when she saw a news segment flash across the screen of the television on the wall behind Mrs. Doles' head.

The television was muted, but subtitles scrolled across the screen beneath the man speaking. "My name is Harold Fitzgerald, coming to you with a breaking news report of a missing girl in the Delta Ridge area. Miss Cross, whose picture is shown here, was involved in illegal activities early this morning and will likely be traveling under an assumed name. Do not approach. If you see this girl or have any information, please contact your local law enforcement. My name is Harold Fitzgerald, channel two news." Matrix stared in shock as the words scrolled across the screen.

Mrs. Doles waited as the girl appeared almost ready to accept her offer. But just as she believed that she had gotten through, there was a sudden shift in the girl's demeanor. Just as Mrs. Doles was turning to see what had stolen the girl's attention, she bolted.

Matrix took advantage of her opportunity the second Mrs. Doles' attention moved away from her. She darted past the lady and her children just as the final words were scrolling from the television screen. She slammed through the café door, startling the bell into motion and loudly announcing her exit. It had just gotten a lot more difficult to hide in her new world. The picture that was used in the news alert was the one from her file, so whoever was after her knew who she was. And worst of all, Varian Ledger was actually her real name, she thought in annoyance.

Outside of the café, Matrix hesitated. She had no idea which way to go from here, and she would not get a second chance if she chose wrong.

Taking a deep breath, she forced herself to think clearly and evaluate her surroundings. She was in the middle of nowhere. There was a small gravel lot off to her right, the town to her left, and a road a short distance in front of her and past the lot. With little information to base her decision on, she picked the path that headed out of town as her best shot and started briskly walking in that direction. She heard the café door open behind her but didn't stop to look. There was no time to look back, she needed to get of out here now. It was more than just the café, she needed to leave her entire life behind. There was no point in looking to the past now, there was nothing there for her anymore.

Matrix increased her pace as she neared the road. She was desperate to escape the eyes she could feel on her retreating form. It was the second time that day that she had ran from someone offering to help her, but she steeled herself against the onslaught of emotions and forced herself to continue, resisting the voice that told her to run back to the kind lady from the café. She had almost made it past the lot, but when she neared the final vehicle, a sleek, black SUV, a single man in a black suit stepped out of the driver's seat. Matrix's eyes automatically began scanning him for weapons while simultaneously reaching for one of her own and searching for the best way out. The tall man in the neatly pressed suit had closely cut, light brown hair and wore a serious expression, but his eyes were concealed behind a dark pair of sunglasses. Matrix never trusted anyone in sunglasses. The eyes can offer so much information about a person before they ever open their mouth. They can show love and trust or fear and malice. With the eyes covered, a person can hide their true intentions with much greater ease. She often wore them herself for that very reason.

As the man approached her at a deliberate rate, Matrix stopped her forward momentum and stood her ground. Her stance was defensive, but not openly hostile as she leveled the man with a steely gaze.

"Good afternoon, Miss Cross," the man greeted jovially in a British accent.

Matrix was silently gathering as much information from the man as possible. The way he carried himself spoke of a military background, his accent placed him near the London area, and his shoes were more expensive than most. With that information, Matrix could guess that he was working with someone on the more shady side of the government, with international reach, and willing to pay for the best. That likely meaning that this man would be good at what he does and was not to be underestimated. Well if they sent him after her, assuming they knew about the Phoenixes, they would have to send someone good. Not that she was bragging, but her team does… did have an impressive track record.

Not wanting to give anything away, Matrix kept her questions simple. "Who do you work for and what do you want?" she asked darkly before the man could continue his introduction.

The man standing across from her smirked at the question. "Well, not one for chit chat I see," he said, smiling broadly, but seeing the mirthless expression on Matrix's face, he hummed consentingly, "Very well, down to business." "I am here representing an international group simply known as The Organization or The Org. as most of us call it."

Matrix crossed her arms offering him an unimpressed look and a raised eyebrow that clearly told him to speed up the story. She had already gathered most of that, but the name of her enemy might prove useful.

The man in the suit sighed again, "Miss Cross, I am sure you have already thought up a hundred different ways to kill me, but I am willing to bet you won't."

Matrix let out a short laugh at the cocky remark. Bold of him to challenge her. "And why is that?" she asked contemptuously.

The man in the suit took two slow, threatening steps forward, "Because I have something you want," he whispered, now looming over Matrix. "Or should I say, someone you want," his sweet accent dropping an octave for a more threatening tone.

A chill ran down her spine, eliciting a sharp but nearly inaudible intake of breath before Matrix could fully shutdown the reflex. The brief moment of transparency was all the man needed for confirmation. Matrix knew that any attempts at denying her interest in the man's implications would be useless at this point. It was a rookie mistake and this man was good enough to notice it. Even with everything that had been on her mind today, she would not be able to forgive herself for the small telling mistake.

The Brit's smirk intensified, "Now that I have your attention, I believe you also have something that I want."

Matrix instantly knew what he was talking about, but also knew the implications. Time to gather a little more information. "So, how long ago did you manage to infiltrate the base?" she deadpanned, "Since it appears you know who I am and about my team, I'm willing to bet a while." Matrix mentally gauged his reaction, wishing again that he would remove the sunglasses. There was no obvious reaction, so she decided to prod a bit more. "If you were there before Project Marionette, then that was not your original mission," she continued, noticing a slight twitch of his hand at the mention of Marionette. "Ah, so you definitely know about Project Marionette. But you were not able to secure the device yourself," she instigated with a subtle smile. "I would have expected more from the Org.," Matrix added sarcastically and waited for his reaction.

His mistake was immediate. "We weren't trying. Had we been, trust me there would have been no need for this conversation," the man in the suit shot back defensively.

Matrix dramatically lifted an eyebrow, "Oh, you were not even aware of the device." "Shame on your organization," she continued in a mock scolding tone.

By that point, the man's smirk had transformed into an expression of anger, but he realized what she was doing. "Just hand it over sweetheart, and we can all get what we want," he muttered patronizingly.

"You expect me to fall for that," Matrix laughed, "If you were watching my team before finding out about Marionette, then obviously we were your initial interest." "And, I doubt your superiors are going to let us go so easily," she concluded with a wink.

"You make a fair point sweetheart. We aren't going to let you get away that easily, so you really should hand it over and come with me before this gets messy," the man threatened, pulling back the edge of his blazer to reveal a sleek 45.

"I'm afraid getting the device out safely was not my top priority. As we have already established," Matrix added with a shrug.

Clearly irritated, the man in the suit took one more step forward, discreetly pressing his gun into her side. "I will ask one last time. Come with me or he dies," was the deep, resonating threat.

Sighing, Matrix took a quick step around the man, lightly giggling to herself as the man rushed to conceal his exposed weapon from unwanted eyes.

The Org. representative whipped around angrily and watched baffled as Matrix sauntered into the back seat of his vehicle.

Matrix could feel the suspicion coming off the man in waves as he climbed into the driver's seat, but to his credit, he didn't comment about her decision to sit in the back. He was smart not to trust her, but honestly, what did she have to lose at this point?

CHAPTER 15

Reunion

The drive was long and awkward. Neither occupant of the vehicle trusted the other. The man in the suit, or "Suit Man" as Matrix had now dubbed him, searched her for weapons before starting the engine, but they both knew he had not found them all, she thought with a smile.

Matrix had stuffed Project Marionette unceremoniously between the seats before Suit Man came to search her or take her bag. It would buy her a little time until she decided what to do with it.

It had already been dark for a while and they were still driving. Matrix leaned her head over against the window, letting her gaze drift upward. She was in no rush to meet her next overlord, and an opportunity to stare at the stars uninterrupted was rare under Dr. Jamison's control. With Dr. Jamison out of the way, Matrix knew what their first use of Project Marionette was likely to be. They would use it to recondition her team, and this time remove their ability to rebel. No more free will. All she had accomplished was trading one prison for another. She could only hope that this one would not turn out to be run by another psychopath determined to rebel and exact his revenge. Matrix sighed heavily settling back into the car seat to watch the stars in the sky.

As she allowed her muscles to relax, it came crashing back to her that it had been nearly two days since she had slept. Well, adrenaline has a way of making it seem that trivial details like that shouldn't matter. But knowing that this was likely her last chance to rest uninterrupted and that it was unlikely this man would try to kill her before attempting to extract as much information as possible, she allowed her eyes to drift closed.

Matrix startled awake, not immediately sure what had awakened her. Being unsure of her surroundings, Matrix willed her body to stay still, feigning sleep until she could properly assess her situation. It was a defense mechanism drilled into them early on. In the event of being captured, a lot of useful information could be gathered while the captors believe their hostage is not listening. Matrix had heard entire plans divulged in front of a seemingly unconscious prisoner, only to have the prisoner escape with the knowledge a few short hours later. That prisoner may or may not have been her. As the team member used the most frequently for infiltration, it was only natural that she would have racked up a few captures, but she would argue that most of them were intentional.

The first thing Matrix noticed was that they were still in the car. The sounds of the car's tires on the road were still roaring in the background, but a considerable amount of light managed to pierce through her closed eyelids signaling that she had been asleep for several hours. The man who picked her up must not have come from the place they were headed but rather had been the closest to the base she fled from Matrix deduced. The second thing she noticed was that Suit Man was conversing softly with someone on the phone. It took her sleep muddled mind a moment to catch up, but she realized that this must have been what had awakened her, Matrix focused her attention on listening in to what was being said. Suit Man kept his voice low, likely in an attempt not to wake his passenger and to keep his conversation private. *Well, nice try, but too late for that*, Matrix thought, smiling subtlety to herself. Matrix had to listen closely to make out the voice of the man on the other end of the line, and most of what he said was lost in the low hum of the tires on the road. Suit Man on the other hand was no challenge to understand. His posh accent floated effortlessly through the space in the SUV, reaching her sensitive ears and bringing with it the information she was seeking.

"Yes, sir. She's sleeping in the back seat right now," Suit Man boasted to his superior. Something something "came so easily?" the other man asked. Suit man seemed to consider the question for a moment before answering. "Honestly, she seemed fairly lackadaisical about the whole thing. Only thing that got any real reaction was the mention of her partner. She seemed pretty surprised," Suit Man responded.

The mention of her previous slip caused Matrix to cringe internally, but she continued to listen.

Something "good to know" something something "base" something.

This was starting to get frustrating Matrix decided as the car hit another patch of obnoxiously loud pavement.

"We are about an hour out, sir," Suit Man responded to what must have been a question regarding their ETA. Something "hood?" no "good" something "other three" something "anxious" something "see her," the muffled words drifted out of the speaker, "Good work," Nathan or Nelson or maybe Mason? That must be Suit Man's actual name Matrix decided. There was another short, formal exchange of goodbyes, that for that most part, Matrix didn't bother trying to interpret.

After their goodbyes, the man on the other end seemed to remember something that triggered a short but much more hushed discussion, at the end of which Suit Man promptly ended the call. With the few words she could decipher, Matrix was able to piece together that she was being taken to the Organization's main base and that they were holding the rest of her team there. The last bit of their conversation was much more difficult to interpret, but she believed it was something to do with Project Marionette. The most shocking part of the phone call for Matrix was to hear that they were holding multiple Phoenixes. Suit Man had implied that they were holding Blade, but she had not expected them to have recovered Corbet or Ivy.

As she sat in the back seat of the SUV at the mercy of her driver, Matrix couldn't help but feel a knot of panic form in her stomach. When it was just a threat, she could deny it with a large enough fraction of her mind to force herself not to care what was happening, but now that she heard them discussing the others without knowing that she was listening, there was no room for denial. She was relieved to hear that Blade had made it out, even if he was captured. He was the only ally that she had left, but what about Corbet and Ivy? She and Blade had betrayed them. They literally fought them and left them in that base to die. Of course, they had no way of knowing at the time that their actions would trigger the base to self-destruct, but how were they going to explain that to them? And they did not even give them a choice to join with the plan. But that would have been such a huge risk. The odds were not in favor of the desired outcome if they had been asked to join. It was necessary to act before they were prepared for the attack.

As much as Matrix tried to convince herself that she and Blade had made the right decision, the more difficult it became to stay in control of her emotions. Honestly, she would never know what would have happened had she given Corbet and Ivy the option to join them, but now, in their eyes, it would be her and Blade that betrayed them, not Dr. Jamison.

Not wanting Suit Man to know that she had been listening to his conversation, Matrix chose to continue pretending she was asleep. She could use the time to come up with a plan for when they arrive at the Organization's base. *Seriously, they couldn't have come up with a more creative name than "the Organization?"*

Back in the cell with Major Lockfire, Blade was making his best attempt to set the back of the Major's head on fire with his eyes. Major Lockfire had been on the phone with someone for the past twenty-two minutes and thirty-five seconds when he finally dropped the phone and returned it to his pocket. The Major nonchalantly moved to stand in front of the glass cells again. Major Lockfire smiled mockingly at Blade's heated expression. "Now you know it's not polite to stare," he quipped in Blade's direction. But the teen's stare only intensified, if that was even possible, and he jerked violently at his restraints. The Major laughed at the frustrated attempts of his captives. "Come now, you should be happy. I have good news," he proclaimed looking between each of the Phoenixes. When he received no response from the three teens, he dropped his shoulders dramatically simultaneously letting out an exasperated sigh. "You guys are no fun," he pouted, still teasing his captives. "Fine," he continued in an overly dramatic voice, "I just received a call, it seems a friend of yours will be joining us soon."

Major Lockfire smiled as he finally received the response he was looking for. The two teens on the sides seemed surprised but otherwise unimpressed. However, the raven-haired boy in the middle's eyes went marginally wide before narrowing again. The Major could detect a mixture of surprise, anger, and sorrow mixed into the slightly deflated glare that was still being pinned on him. That is what he was looking for. The entire process would prove much easier if he could manage to take a bit of the fight out of his newest assets first.

By the time Matrix and Suit Man had reached the base, Matrix had decided that she was not going to allow the Organization to use her the way Dr. Jamison had. At least not without giving them a heck of a fight.

Hearing confirmation that they were holding Blade meant that this was not just about her anymore. He had taken just as many risks as her by turning against Jamison. She owed it to him to at least try to prevent them from being placed right back under someone else's control.

With her defiant spark reignited, Matrix took it upon herself to destroy Project Marionette. Matrix carefully worked the device out from between the seat cushions and concealed it in her lap, careful to make sure that Suit Man did not notice. She rolled the metal sphere over a few times in her hands, trying to determine the best way to bypass the sturdy outer casing. With the device disconnected from its power source, the grooves that had previously been emitting the icy blue light were now dormant. As Matrix examined the device, she couldn't help but find it difficult to believe that the small device was capable of interfering with neural pathways or implanting memories. In its dormant state, the small device had a deceptively innocent appearance in her opinion. However, it unfortunately did appear to be made quite sturdy. All of the seams in the metal were carefully smoothed and fit precisely into alignment. It was going to be difficult to do a significant amount of damage with her limited tools. Ultimately, Matrix decided that the small panel where the device would be connected to a power source was the weakest point and likely to be her best option.

Suit Man had searched her well, but he neglected to remove the two solid black snap bracelets that she was wearing, one on each wrist. Matrix removed the bracelet from her left wrist and carefully controlled the piece of metal back into a straight piece in order to prevent the signature snapping sound. Once it was straightened out, she slipped the black cover off the bracelet. While a snap bracelet would generally be made from thin, flimsy metal and rounded at both ends, Matrix's unassuming bracelets uncurled to form a sharp, sturdy metal knife. It would not be her first choice for the job since they were still somewhat difficult to work with, but they often went unnoticed, making them the perfect way to smuggle in a weapon.

Matrix flipped the weapon over so that it would not roll up when she used it to pry open the panel and went to work.

The design of the device made Matrix's job slow and difficult. They were rapidly approaching the base, and Matrix knew she had very little time to complete the task. Once she pried open the panel, several wires were revealed. She cut each of the wires and began pulling apart the small pieces accessible through the small hole. It was not going to be enough. She may have bought them some time, but if these people are as smart as she thinks they will be, then they will be able to repair the device. Quickly, she pulled out as many of the inner components as she could in search of the control panel circuit board. Matrix was ignorant of the small shocks delivered to her fingers as the remaining energy in the device was expelled into her body. There was no time to give it any of her attention, and it was nothing compared to her training. Matrix spared a glance up to determine how much time she had left before she would be discovered and was not happy with what she saw. They were rapidly approaching the base, and she would have loved to be able to assess it before entering. But, she only had thirty seconds tops, and Project Marionette was her top priority. Matrix hastily grabbed a circuit board with multiple important chips attached and pulled it free from the device. Taking her snap bracelet knife again, she pried several of the chips free. With the base quickly closing in, she quietly shoved the broken device back between the seat cushions, with the exception of a couple of important-looking chips.

Matrix was not satisfied with her work. She could hope that it would take them some time to discover her hiding place, but the device was not beyond repair.

"Here we are, princess," Suit Man loudly announced, likely still believing that she was asleep. Matrix's head snapped up at the sudden sound, glaring at Suit Man in the rear-view mirror. "What's wrong, princess? Didn't get enough beauty sleep?" he jabbed, emphasizing his chipper tone.

Matrix let herself fall back heavily against the seat, carefully disguising a shaky exhale of breath in realization that she had not been caught.

"Well, there's no reason to be sassy about it. After all, I did just spend all night playing your highness's chauffeur," Suit Man continued, misreading her response to his teasing.

Suit Man pulled the SUV up to a checkpoint at the entrance to the base, and a very professional acting young guard came up the window to verify Suit Man had the proper clearance. Matrix leaned forward to peer through the windshield while the two conversed. The base was extensive, but she memorized every detail in an attempt to gather as much information as possible. Sometimes it was surprising how a small piece of information could end up saving your life later. However, while studying the base, she never turned her full attention away from the two men conversing. Absently she noticed the name on the ID that Suit Man showed was indeed Nelson, Anthony Nelson.

The two men had a short, curt exchange that resulted in the man shining a light into the back of the vehicle where Matrix was sitting. Matrix crossed her arms and stuck her tongue out at the guard before winking defiantly and rebelliously directing her eyes to face straight ahead. The guard only looked over the girl unperturbed before nodding to the driver and motioning him through. But, Matrix liked to think that inside she had gotten some kind of response from the guard. If nothing else, maybe a bit of confusion. She could certainly have that effect on people when she wanted.

Suit Man, as Matrix was still choosing to call him, continued to ramble on as they drove up to the up to the base. However, Matrix paid little attention to his attempts at arousing a reaction from her. Instead, she chose to further evaluate both the base and the guards, looking for any patterns or data that could be useful later.

Matrix felt the SUV slow to a stop in front of the massive base. The large gray building had a much more sophisticated appearance than most of the military bases she had encountered on past missions. The security from the outside was prevalent, but that was not what caught her attention. There was a twelve-foot, chain link, gated fence around the perimeter that stood an impressive ninety yards from the building. That would leave a lot of open ground to cover before reaching the fence. The top of the fence was adorned with coils of concertina wire, and as they passed through, Matrix noticed a sign warning that it was electrified. There were also several guard stations positioned strategically around the base with the bulk of the guards positioned at the checkpoint at the entrance gate. A slight challenge perhaps but definitely doable. Ok, next, cameras. Each guard station had a security camera with night vision capabilities, there were cameras on each of the irregular corners along the perimeter of the base, and finally, a camera pointed at each of the doors that were visible.

Matrix remained completely unreadable as two heavily

armed guards dragged her from the back of the SUV with a hand on each of her elbows. However, her gaze drifted up to one of the cameras. Matrix stared directly into the lens, knowingly looking into the eyes of the person she knew would be watching her. The mental game was her strong suit. As she turned her attention back to her present situation, she replaced the vacant expression on her face. Looking at the camera had provided her some additional information. A small red light was illuminated at the bottom of the circular lens that was not lit on any of the other cameras that were farther off. Motion-activated, she concluded. Not uncommon but not the standard either. No, it was the panels on the building that caught her attention. She couldn't be sure what their purpose was, but she counted four and noted their position for later.

The guards briefly spoke with her driver as a formality, then began leading her into the base. Matrix didn't resist, it wasn't time to make her move yet. She needed to see the others first, and it was best to keep her captors off guard for as long as possible.

"Have a nice stay, Princess," Suit Man called, smirking mischievously at her.

Matrix froze briefly, straightening her back, but resisted acknowledging the infuriating Brit any further. The guard to her right gave her arm a rough tug that sent her stumbling forward again before she could regain her balance.

The guard that had tugged her forward glanced over at his partner smiling humorously, but their charge gave no reaction. The two silently guided Matrix through the main doors. The inside of the large base where they entered was a modern, open space with an emphasis on glass features and silver accents. It appeared they were bringing her in through the main entrance, an odd choice unless they wanted her to see what she was up against. In front of her, several yards away was an impressive, wide staircase leading up to the next level. Above the staircase, a large seal with the letters O.R.G. proudly displayed. The area was busy with a mix of men and women in both formal attire and field uniforms bustling about. Matrix stiffened as she observed the many unknowns that accompanied being surrounded by the potentially hostile strangers. The guards had paused, assumedly to sign her in, but which offered her the opportunity to take in the expansive complex. To Matrix, it looked as though the building were a strange hybrid of a mall, a military base, and a business firm. Once again, she made note of all the cameras, the armed guards, locks on the doors, and any potential tools she could use later. She was still observing the patterns of the employees when the guards gave her arm another rough tug in the direction of an elevator a short distance to the left. The people they encountered did not spare much more than a glance before returning their focus to their work. Obviously, whoever they were, they were accustomed to prisoners being brought in.

The guard to Matrix's left reached out first to press the button to call the lift. Matrix watched his hand carefully and noticed that he had pressed the down arrow. Briefly, she flashed back the elevators at the base she had just come from and the battle she had fought to escape from the lower levels. The simple action performed by the guard had dragged her mind back into the events she wanted nothing more than to forget. Suddenly, a muted ding signaled that the car had arrived, but Matrix's mind was still catching up as she was pulled from her thoughts and into the lift. She shook her head subtly in an attempt to dispel the lingering anxiety left behind by the memories, but as the doors slid shut behind the trio, Matrix had to fight her instincts to resist the men as the invisible vice around her lungs tightened. A glance at the panel on the inside of the car revealed that there were four levels above ground and two sublevels. Her escorts selected the lowest button, and the car began moving down.

When the doors slid open again, a hallway with harsh white lights and more people going about their business was revealed. Again, the building gave off more of a business feel than a military base. As Matrix began to ponder precisely what she was dealing with, the guards began leading her through a series of turns. One right, pass two turns left, left, and a right. Eventually, they stopped at what looked like a service elevator. The lift was called and again they entered the car. Matrix's eyes instantly went to the buttons on the inside of the car. Unlike before where the floors were labeled 4, 3, 2, G, S1, and S2, this car began at S2 and counted down to 7. *Were there really nine levels underground?* Matrix wondered. The guard pressed the button labeled "5" causing it to illuminate and the car to begin its descent.

When the elevator doors slid open for level five, the atmosphere was distinctly uninviting. There were no people immediately visible and the halls were silent. The ceilings were much lower, and the lights were spaced much farther apart, causing the space to appear much dimmer than the previous parts of the base she had seen. Considering the less than friendly invitation she had received from Suit Man, Matrix deduced that this must be the level they used for holding prisoners. The claustrophobic feeling of the low ceilings and narrow halls mixed with the low lighting was likely intended to psychologically affect those being held here. It was as though she had been transported to somewhere much less friendly than the simply cold and impersonal levels above. In response, Matrix instinctually set her mind to filter out any of the responses her captors were likely trying to evoke and instead placed herself in a purely objective state of mind. She often found it easier to resist giving in to her interrogators when all emotion was removed. Fear, pain, and persuasion became much less tangible, easier to ignore. It was like disconnecting from reality, so that only the objective remained. And failure was no longer an option.

Matrix's analysis of her situation was complete in a matter of seconds. While stepping out of the lift to the sound of an annoyed guard grunting something akin to the word "move," she had already gathered all the data available to her in the hallway. Anything from the distance each direction from the lift to the number of lightbulbs to the scratches on the floor was neatly filed away in her mind. She continued to catalog each turn they made until they came to a halt before a large metal door. Her mind was attuned to every detail with nothing escaping. Door, medium gray, steel, one hundred seventy-six scratches, (obviously not a good part of town), full-length hinges on the right side in twenty-four segments, black scuffs at the bottom peaking twelve times, (obviously they do not mop the floors very well) bits of debris clinging to the bottom, (really selling the torture chamber vibes) a small rectangular window approximately 41 centimeters tall and 10 centimeters at the bottom, three-centimeter diamond-shaped chain link in addition to the glass, thumbprint on the lower right corner of the glass but otherwise it was clean. Surprisingly, it would appear they do clean something down here, but what likely happened was the man cleaning the window slipped because the floors were still damp from his sad attempt at mopping and had to brace his hand against the door. The height and size of the print confirmed that it was a man approximately five feet ten inches tall and the angle of the print confirmed that was likely bracing himself. That coupled with the mop fibers mixed in with the debris clinging to the door help to confirm her hypothesis, and she noted a janitor on the first level that was the proper height. What else? She noted the seams around the window, speculated the purpose of the window, and analyzed everything visible on the other side of the glass. Then there was the door handle. There are so many things one can observe in a simple handle, or not so simple in this case. There were simple aspects like the color which was suited to the door but three shades lighter. The wear on the handle, with visible marks of a right thumb and left thumb grip which indicated that it had been used frequently by both a right-handed person and a left-handed person. All the way down to the handle's innermost mechanisms, why that design might have been chosen and what that says about the one who chose it, and the quality of the bolts securing it in place. She took in everything. Not because she wanted to, but simply because that was how her mind functioned. It had become natural, and it was part of why she had been selected to be a Phoenix in the first place.

The guard on Matrix's left released her arm in favor of unlocking the door. His keys were in his right hand and the left was placed on the handle. This was not the left-handed man, and she had noticed the other guard sign in with his right. There was someone else who frequented the room they were preparing to enter that she had yet to meet. However, she was certain that she would find out soon enough.

Major Lockfire's attention was drawn away from his three guests by the sound of the door being unlocked a few meters behind him. The Major brought his palms together in a sign of anticipation. "It would seem your teammate has finally arrived," the Major informed the three prisoners before facing the door.

All eyes were on the large steel door as it slowly creaked open. The tension hung heavily in the air as three figures emerged from behind the gray shield. Two large men were guiding their reluctant but begrudgingly cooperative charge. The young girl's eyes quickly scanned over the occupants in the cells, hovering on the middle for just a moment longer, before settling on Major Lockfire. Once fully inside, the room with the door once again locked, the two men snapped to attention jerking the girl straighter in-between them. Major Lockfire inspected his men briefly, then waved a dismissive hand, and the two settled. He was much more interested in the shortest of the trio and paid little attention to the other two. "Good morning, Miss Cross," the Major greeted with a genuine smile. "It's so nice of you to join us," he said gesturing to the other three Phoenixes.

Matrix continued to pin the Major under an unreadable gaze. These repressed children were really starting to get on his nerves. Eventually, he would get something out of them. He had seen it a couple of times, he just needed to find the right buttons to push. Nothing was more fun than irritating the crap out of a captive.

Major Lockefire began to pace in front of Matrix and the Phoenixes in their cells. "You know, Miss Cross. I was intrigued when my associate that picked you up told me how you just climbed into his vehicle without a fight. I was wondering if you would mind explaining to me and my new friends, why a respectable girl such as yourself would do that," he asked, pausing his pacing and looking her in the eye. He had drawn the attention of everyone in the room, but Matrix stood motionless with her chin held high and eyes matching the Major's. "No explanation for yourself?" the Major asked continuing his one-sided conversation. Again, nothing but an emotionless stare met his question. "You should know that I have all of your files right here; Cross, Matrix, file number 0076228-0582. I know everything there is to know about you," the Major said threateningly looking directly at each Phoenix, "There is no reason to hide things from me. In fact, it will be much easier for all of us if you don't."

He had their files. Matrix realized that she must have been right about the Org. infiltrating Dr. Jamison's base long before learning about Project Marionette. Under different circumstances, it would have been relieving to hear. All records of their pasts had assumedly burned along with the base, but now she knew that copies existed. And she was standing in the same room as the man who had access to them.

Matrix's eyes resumed following the Major as he paced the distance of the room once again. "Matrix," he began sweetly, "I expected this from those three, but you? You are supposed to be the one that is good with people, infiltrating circles, gathering information, and just speaking in general," he summarized, waving his hands around to make his point before dropping them to his sides.

Matrix hesitated for a moment, and the corner of her mouth twitched up into a small crooked smile. "There are a lot of ways to gather information, Major," Matrix finally answered in a low, smooth voice.

The Major appeared caught off guard for a moment, apparently no longer expecting her to respond. Matrix's lips spread into an open smile, "You are down here a lot, aren't you, Major?" There was a hint of a humorless laugh behind her words as she gauged his reaction.

Major Lockfire's eyes snapped up to meet her face with a spark of anger barely concealed behind them. His mouth slightly open, poised to speak, but Matrix beat him to it.

"You like being down here, don't you, Major?" Matrix continued, trying to get in his head. "You like feeling in control over others. It makes you feel powerful, important, unbeatable," she took a slow, deliberate step toward the Major, "but you can't stand it when they are giving you orders. Who are they to tell you what to do? You are so much smarter than them. That's why you come here." Matrix tilted her head slightly while taking another slow step forward.

The Major was transfixed on the girl, his lips parted and quivering but with no words coming out.

It was getting easier to get in the Major's head, and she had his undivided attention.

"Sir?" Matrix heard one of the guards behind her say, but the Major was too absorbed in her words to notice.

"You enjoy breaking people, seeing the pain on their faces as they tell you everything you want to know." Her voice remained low and smooth, like silk or the voice of a serial killer cooing to their next victim as their thumb delicately wipes a tear from the cheek of the helpless muse. "You resented having to answer to that man's orders, didn't you?" she asks conspiratorially, "Major Lockfire." The last part was added on effortlessly, almost as an afterthought and as casually as if to an old friend, but the effect was staggering.

The Major sucked in a sharp breath, "H-how did you know?"

Matrix smiled devilishly. She had recognized his voice as soon as he spoke. Colonel Redborn radioed in to one of his men on the base, she had heard the name just as she slipped away to gather supplies from her room. But, looking at the Major it was as though she had just read his mind, and she saw no reason to break the illusion.

"Put her in the cell," the Major ordered abruptly, extending his finger to point to the last empty cell.

Matrix smiled internally at the slight tremor in the visibly shaken Major's hand.

Even as the two guards pulled her toward the cell at the end of the row behind her, she kept her eyes fixated on the Major over her shoulder. One of the guards scanned his card and the other roughly shoved the girl inside. Her hand caught his belt, and she giggled as he had to take a step to recover his balance. She turned with her hands clasped behind her back and chin down peering through her eyelashes as the door slid closed behind her. "Say hello to Snowball for me, Major," she called to Major Lockfire's back as he stormed out of the room.

Abruptly, the Major froze whipping around to see Matrix smiling at him innocently. But as suddenly as his motion ceased, the spell was broken, and he turned rushing from the room followed by the guards.

Once certain they were out of hearing range, one of the guards strode up to the Major. "Didn't you once say you have a cat named Snowball, Sir?" the guard asked hesitantly.

Major Lockfire swallowed thickly, nodding his head but never making eye contact. The guard lingered in step with the major for a moment unsure if he would say more, but when he gave no indication of doing so, the guard excused himself and returned to his duties.

The Major mulled over everything that Matrix had said in the holding room, trying to make sense of it all. He was not one to spook easily, but it felt as though she had been inside his mind and began voicing his innermost thoughts. Thoughts that had begun to scare him as he heard them aloud. Her sweet voice echoed through his thoughts as he walked without a destination. He had rushed from the room without a clear destination in mind, his only goal being to get away from the girl and gather his composure. Most startling was how effortlessly she had spoken not only his name but the name of his cat! Her file was quite impressive, but how could she possibly have known? The Major did not like having people in his head. Next time he would need to be careful, very careful.

Matrix watched as the door closed and she was left alone with her team. She was not naïve enough to believe that they were truly alone. A base as advanced as this one was certain to have several hidden cameras and microphones in its confinement cells.

She didn't always enjoy getting into the minds of her enemy, but the arrogant Major... Well, it had been a pleasure. He had made it almost too easy. He was so determined to provoke a reaction from her that he let his guard down. His name had been easy, she recognized his voice from Colonel Redborn's radio, but he didn't know that. Matrix had also noticed his clipped tone when he answered the Colonel. Yes, he had been under a lot of pressure when the Colonel contacted him, but Matrix had noticed an undercurrent of annoyance, almost resentment, in his voice when he acknowledged the Colonel. He was also proud and overconfident in himself. He stood with his shoulders back, prodding his captives, and wanting to make sure they knew he was the one in control. It was likely he had a significant, overbearing figure in his life which led to him resent authority. A military father perhaps. She had also noticed that his primary weapon was holstered on his left side. A solid indicator that he was left-handed. That coupled with the noticeable wear on the door handle from a left-handed man and his reactions as she spoke, made it natural to then conclude that the Major was the one frequently visiting these cells.

Matrix had a gift for reading people, and once the Major was caught off guard, it was no challenge to put her skills to work. The funniest part though, was when she mentioned his cat on the way out. Determining he had a pet was the easy part. He had obviously made an effort to keep his uniform clean, but white fur on a black uniform, no matter how little, was hard to miss. With the length of the fur and most of the fur being concentrated in a pattern around his ankles, guessing he had a cat was not that big of a leap. The name on the other hand had been an educated guess.

After thoroughly freaking out the Major, Matrix figured she had bought herself some margin for error. The Major looked as though he was in his early thirties, maybe thirty-two, and had likely dedicated himself to the military at a young age before joining the Organization. Sighing, Matrix realized she still needed to uncover exactly who the Organization was. There were several strong military connections, but it was nothing like the typical military groups she had encountered in the past. The Major may even have joined the Org. out of spite toward his father, but now Matrix was beginning to believe that was nearly as much speculation as guessing his cat's name. She had noticed a small amount of fur that was a slightly different color than the rest. Gray fur, she had concluded. With the Major being relatively young, it was likely that he had had the senior cat for many years, probably before joining the military. With the average lifespan of a cat being fifteen years, it was likely that he named the cat at a young age. *Snowball is a very common name for white cats*, Matrix concluded laughing to herself. It was mostly luck that she had been led to the correct name.

Getting into the mind of another person was one of Matrix's more useful skills, but not one that she took lightly. She enjoyed reading those around her, figuring out who they are, and what their intentions were. It was a gift that had served her well during her career, but it certainly had its risks and a dark side. As a child she was tasked with entering the mind of the enemy, learning how to think like them, predict their actions, and become one of them. It was necessary for her role on the team, to successfully infiltrate the other side, but it was no longer something she did for pleasure.

Her team dealt with many deranged men, from mercenaries to military leaders. Each time she studied a new person, she took on their traits and pattern of thought. It was like becoming a new person, completely separate from herself, each time. Early in her training, she had the tendency to go too deep into the role and it became difficult to separate herself from the persona. Countless times she had found herself unable to isolate the thoughts that were her own from thoughts that her mind had filled in from another's perspective. It was difficult to retain what her original personality had been and what was assimilated from those she had studied. Through the years, Dr. Jamison had worked to balance her ability. He forced her to fully immerse herself in the psyche of countless men and women, only to pull her away once she fell too deep. Each time it became easier to become another person, but she never forgot how it felt to feel herself slip away and someone else take her place.

It was as though she could feel their emotions building up inside her, with no escape and no idea why she was experiencing them. She was taught from a young age to eliminate her emotions unless they were useful, but when mimicking another person it became much more difficult to remain objective when her mind was behaving as if she were the other person and flooding her mind with emotions that were foreign to her thought processes. She could feel what they felt. Their pain, their fear, their rage, it all became a part of her in a way that made it feel as though it was her own. She was becoming the person so completely that it felt as though she was slipping away in the process. Flashes of thoughts that were barely recognizable as her own creation began pouring down like rain in a cyclone, overwhelming her mind until she was forced to break the persona or risk losing herself in the storm. How could someone ever forget that kind of experience?

By the time she was ten, Matrix had over one hundred different personas she could pull from to fit her situation. Sometimes it still became difficult to determine where she ended and the act began. She had been exposed to thoughts no child her age ever should have but had to compartmentalize what was needed for the mission and bend it to her will. That is what she had done to Major Lockfire. She came in without a file on the man's background, but he had given her everything she needed. Staring deep into one's eyes could have a strong psychological effect. One that Matrix was skilled in manipulating. His full attention was on her and she had used his vulnerability and his body language to read his thoughts. Something she would always enjoy was seeing the faces of men as they had their innermost thoughts laid out in front of them as though she had truly entered their minds. She would take the pain from her past. She was grateful for it. Her skills had been earned, and her eyes were opened to a world where she could do the things others only dreamed about, and at least for now, she chose how to use those skills.

CHAPTER 16

Betrayal Can Be a Sign of Respect

Time ticks by slowly when there is nothing but the color of the walls to occupy your mind. Seconds bleed into minutes and minutes bleed into hours. Thoughts become a tangled weave of incomplete threads of ideas and aspirations intersecting and diverging without order. Regrets for the present emerge, mistakes of the past resurface, and hopes for the future form in a futile attempt to reconcile the wavering path which has already been set into motion.

Matrix had been sitting alone with her thoughts for hours with no sign of an end. The dim, artificial light of the cell pinned her shadow to the ground in front of her, leaving it no more free than herself. They were too far underground for windows to be of any use which left Matrix reliant on her internal clock for any semblance of day and night. She knew it was all part of the tactics being used to break them. It was just one more subtle way of removing their control and any sense of normal rhythm from their lives.

If she listened closely, she could make out the faint, rhythmic breath of each of her teammates. None of them had spoken since the major left sometime yesterday. A guard had come in shortly after to unshackle the others, but no one had entered since. Again, Matrix found herself wondering if this had all been a mistake. So far, all they had done was trade one cell for another.

Matrix pushed herself up forcefully from the hard cot she had settled on at the back of the room. She paced anxiously across the cell running her hands through her hair. She felt her heart rate spike but couldn't find it in herself to care if she was being irrational. She turned to pace back toward the cot but caught herself mid-step and abruptly spun slamming her fists into the glass behind her. She was done waiting for the others to realize that they needed each other if they were going to get out of this.

She stood at the glass wall of her cell mouth half-open poised to speak, but when the moment came, the words would not come. What could she say to them? At the end of the day, she and Blade had left them to ensure that their own escape would be successful. The success of the mission always comes first. That is what Dr. Jamison had preached to them since the beginning of their training. Surely Corbet and Ivy above anyone else could understand that, but now it just didn't feel right. Loyalty had not been at the top of Dr. Jamison's list when it came to anyone other than himself. Attachment was a liability. If a Phoenix is lost in the field, it is their own responsibility to free themself. He had taught them everything they needed to know to survive capture, but there would be no cavalry coming to save them. Ironically, his principles were what led Matrix to justify betraying her teacher. There were no exceptions to his rules, so it became easier to extend those rules to Dr. Jamison himself.

Matrix took a deep breath. She knew the others were listening and waiting for her to say something. Blade would likely back whatever she said, after all, they were in this together. Corbet, he would listen to logic. If she made a good case, he would go along if it was in his best interest. Ivy on the other hand was much more unpredictable, she was much more likely to hold a grudge, and considering their past rivalry... Well, she would be much harder to convince and certainly not trustworthy. *Trustworthy*, Matrix scoffed to herself, none of them were trustworthy.

"You betrayed us," Ivy spoke in a level voice brimming with barely controlled rage.

Her words were so sudden in the vast silence that Matrix flinched as though they had struck her. Matrix froze, a new heavier silence settling around the room. She had not expected Ivy to make the first move. What could she say to that? It was true. She had betrayed both Corbet and Ivy. There was no point in denying that. Matrix raised her head and stared at the solid wall that divided her from her team. Her eyes settled at eye level with Ivy even though they could not see each other through the barrier. "Yes," she replied simply.

"You betrayed us," Ivy repeated more forcefully sounding angrier and annoyed.

It was not a question, but Matrix could sense that there was more intent behind her words. An unspoken message that it seemed she believed that Matrix should already know. Matrix was careful to keep all emotion from her voice as she spoke again, "Yes, I did."

This time, Matrix heard a dull thud followed by a squeak that sounded painfully like someone strangling a mouse as Ivy punched her cot and rose to stand. Matrix tracked her footsteps, subconsciously following Ivy in her mind.

"You know they are listening to us," Ivy snapped, allowing more of her anger to spill into her words.

"Yes," Matrix confirmed, her tone cold and calculated. There was no point for remorse over what happened between them. Soon enough, Ivy would come to terms with the fact that they needed each other. Until then, Matrix would allow Ivy to release anything she felt that she needed to say. Ivy was known for her outbursts, but she was on the team for a reason. She always got the job done... regardless of the costs.

"You expect us to help you now, don't you?" Ivy asked, crossing her arms defensively.

Her words were harsh and accusing. Matrix knew the point she was trying to make. *You got all of us into this mess and now you expect us to get you out.* This would be so much easier if she could show Ivy the files that she and Blade had discovered. "Do either of us have a choice?" Matrix asked calmly.

"Do we have a choice!" Ivy exclaimed barely below a shout, "You had a choice before any of this began!"

"I..." Matrix began, but she was cut off before she could say anymore.

"No! You betrayed all of us, especially Dr. Jamison!" Ivy condemned.

Matrix cringed at the mention of Jamison. If anyone had betrayed them, it was him. He had used them. Yes, he made them powerful, skilled operatives, and she was grateful for that. But he had still used them, and for that, he paid with his life. "You didn't know him like I did," Matrix said quietly, a hint of disappointment in her voice, "He lied to us." "He used you," Matrix continued, emphasizing each word.

"He saved us!" Ivy screamed pounding her palm into the glass, "Don't you dare try to turn us against him! I will kill you!" Ivy's amber eyes sparkled with rage, and her olive cheeks flushed red.

Sadly, Matrix understood her anger all too well. When she stopped thinking logically, she felt that same anger directed at herself as much as Jamison. They were brainwashed by him, conditioned to be loyal to him alone, and completely obedient without question. Every second a voice that sounded just like Jamison was screaming at her that she was wrong. It was so ingrained into each of them that it was second nature to look to him for instruction. They were not supposed to make decisions on their own. Every aspect of their thoughts, actions, and emotions were to be dictated to them by Dr. Jamison. Good or evil, they all lost their sense of direction and purpose in that explosion. It would be a while before any of them learned what that was going to mean moving forward. But, it was also not in her nature to back down from a fight. Regardless of who was challenging her.

"I would like to see you try. You didn't do too well back on the base," Matrix snarked back.

The growl that Ivy let out would have sent most grown men running back to their mothers.

"Girls!" Blade interjected. The two girls had almost forgotten that anyone else was present when Blade summoned their attention. "Just... just stop, will you?" he pleaded with them, "We are stuck in here together, none of this matters anymore."

That's why he was the team leader... if they could still be called a team. He was the voice of reason that kept them all focused on the mission. No matter what, they could depend on him to diffuse the situation and get them working together again.

"Shut it Blade!" Or not... "You went along with that traitor. You are no more innocent in this than she is!" Ivy railed into Blade.

"Listen..." Blade groaned, and the cot creaked under his weight as he sat up.

"No!" Ivy was not in the mood to listen to these two lunatics today, "You two, listen to me!"

Matrix listened to Ivy and Blade argue with each other but was no longer interested in their words.

"Situation report," she requested.

It was posed as a question, and the puzzled tone was out of place in the turbulent atmosphere between the group. Matrix had noticed it when Blade first spoke. His tone was controlled, too controlled. It was as though he wasn't sure that his words would be correct, and he was slightly overcompensating. If Ivy had noticed, she didn't comment. However, Matrix thought it was unlikely considering she probably wasn't able to listen to anyone through her haze of rage... and she is screaming over him Matrix mentally added with an incline of her head.

Blade took a deep breath. He knew exactly what she was asking about.

"Blade?" Matrix prompted again when he didn't immediately answer her.

"I'm fine," he consented, "He wasn't trying to kill me." His voice was rougher than before, an edge of pain not quite as carefully hidden.

Matrix hesitated considering what he had said. That

information could complicate their escape later. "Understood," Matrix acknowledge formally. She was concerned but trusted that he could handle himself and didn't press the issue. The room was quiet for a moment after that, but again, it was Ivy that broke the silence first.

"You are weak," she sneered at Blade, "One of the few mistakes I believe Dr. Jamison ever made was putting you in charge. You never had what it takes to lead a team like this."

Matrix knew that Ivy was just trying to get in their heads and draw them into another rage-fueled argument. It was a classic move of hers, and Matrix knew it well herself. It was much easier to manipulate someone once they were angry and no longer thinking before they spoke.

"And you think you could have done better?" Matrix challenged. She knew that this was not what Ivy was really trying to make a point about. Ivy thought they were traitors, that they had turned against a man who had been everything to them, and she was angry with them for leaving her behind. Watching her world go up in flames had been one of the worst moments of Matrix's life. Ha! Had that life ever really been her own? At that point, nothing had been certain anymore. Arguing with her the other Phoenixes actually helped to restore some sense of normalcy.

"Says the one person who could have been worse," Ivy spat back, drawing Matrix back into the argument. And the argument would have continued if not for a fourth voice joining the room.

"Ladies," Corbet interjected in a mockingly civil tone.

Corbet was a wild card. He was logical but tended to side with his fellow Beta Team member, Ivy. But, if Matrix could sway him, then Ivy was likely to follow.

"Let's hear them out," Corbet said pointedly at Ivy.

Corbet liked to have all of the facts in order to make an

informed decision, but that also meant he wasn't likely to trust them at their word. Words mean nothing. They all knew that. They are the instrument of deception. A hollow promise can be as beautiful and enticing as a Venus flytrap but turn on you the moment you get too close. However, at the moment, words were their only form of communication and any that passed between them risked revealing information to the enemy.

"Do you remember the extra container Blade and I brought back from that weapons recovery mission a few months ago?" Matrix asked in a variant of German.

It was impossible to know how much information the Organization's plants had gathered while on the base, but it would be best to keep their conversations private. The dialect was of Dr. Jamison's creation. It was designed specifically to allow the team to communicate privately when in the presence of others. It was possible that the Org. could decipher their communications, but it would certainly buy them some time.

Matrix recounted the events leading up to her and Blade helping to overtake the base, including all information that she had read on Project Marionette.

"Wait," Corbet interrupted, "you two broke into Dr. Jamison's office?" When there was no denial, he nodded his head approvingly, "Bold move."

Matrix smiled slightly to herself but heard a short laugh from the other side of their private cell block. There was no way to see each other, but it wasn't necessary to tell that Ivy wasn't as easily impressed.

"And where is the device now?" Ivy questioned.

Matrix was reluctant to answer that particular question. She was not exactly proud of her work hiding the device, but she hadn't had many options at the time. So begrudgingly, Matrix continued her story, recounting her attempt to render the device unusable. "For obvious reasons, I am not going to say where the parts are hidden," Matrix said in conclusion. She had left out when the device was destroyed so that, if the Org. managed to translate their conversation, they still would not have its location.

"You made it away?" Blade asked in surprise. They all saw her brought in separately, but he had not known why at the time. He heard what Major Lockfire said, but that was not the same as hearing it from his teammate. "Why would you have let him take you?" Blade asked quietly.

It was a fair question, but one Matrix was not sure how to answer. Logically, she should not have allowed herself to be taken, but in the moment, it didn't seem to matter.

She was comfortable being someone else's weapon. She had fought hard for her freedom, but she had fought for many things not knowing what it would bring. Complete the mission, deal with the consequences later. She had used that same strategy on the base, but this time, she was the one cleaning up the aftermath. It had all been her idea, and when Suit Man or Nelson had told her that Blade and her team were alive, she felt it was her responsibility to protect them.

"Damage control," Matrix answered, switching back to English. There was a lot of meaning in those two words. It was the phrase Dr. Jamison used when a mission failed, and the consequences received for failure were rarely pleasant. She was telling him that she had made a mistake, and this was her punishment.

Blade released a steading stream of breath. You don't spend as much time with someone as they had without getting to know them. "Don't do anything stupid," he warned her.

"And when have I ever done something stupid?" Matrix

asks sarcastically in an attempt to lighten the mood.

Blade didn't laugh. "I'm serious," he said firmly, but his words were laced with concern.

"I know," Matrix replied defensively, but it came off slightly defeated. Matrix knew she had a track record of being reckless, but her risks were always calculated and only when she felt that the situation warranted an extreme response. It may not always appear so from the outside, but she was careful.

"They are probably just confining us here until they can find Marionette," Matrix spoke, trying to direct the attention away from herself.

There was a pause before anyone spoke, and Matrix was concerned that it would not work, but eventually, Blade consented.

"We need to decide what we are doing quickly before that happens," he said resolutely.

Matrix released the breath she hadn't realized she was holding. "Agreed. What can you tell me about what you saw before I got here?" she asked relieved.

"Nothing," Ivy spoke up in her brash tone. "We were all drugged before we got here. I woke up in that chair," she admitted sounding almost embarrassed.

Matrix nodded to herself. She was the only one who knew the layout of the base, so she did her best to descried it for the team.

"This would be so much easier if we could see each other," Ivy whined in frustration.

"Not an option," Corbet stated obviously. There was a loud thud as Ivy's fist contacted the wall dividing her from the next cell.

"Let's just try to focus," Matrix stressed, "We may only get one shot at this."

The team spent the next several hours discussing their best options for escape. It would not be easy. They would all be operating with a dagger behind their back, but if they could stick together long enough to see through the escape, they might have a chance.

CHAPTER 17

On the Edge of Awareness

A single orange-toned light hung in the middle of a dark room. The dim, cone-shaped light swung back and forth like a pendulum flickering and threatening to burn out. Under the light was a rusty, fragile-looking metal chair with two arms and no back. The room, clearly designed to intimidate those unfortunate enough to find themselves there, was in stark contrast to the high-tech feel surrounding the rest of the Organization's base.

Currently, the person unfortunate enough to be seated in that uncomfortable chair, donning a black hood, was Matrix Cross. *They obviously hadn't been too concerned about her escaping*, Matrix thought, testing the strength of her restraints. The cuffs holding her hands in place would have been better suited for a man. She could slip them if she needed to, and they had not even bothered to tie her legs. Honestly, she was a little insulted.

Early that morning, two guards had entered Matrix's cell with a syringe and a hood. First, they had forcefully shoved the hood over her head the way one would when dealing with a feral animal. Next came the needle. Matrix had fought back instinctually as she felt the sharp prick in the bend of her arm. But, as the plunger was depressed, her awareness faded into the darkness of her obscured vision.

Matrix woke an undetermined amount of time later; body slumped forward in the chair and precariously balanced upright. She willed her body to stay still and not alert anyone who may be present that she was awake, just as she had done in the SUV not too long ago. Her mind was still fuzzy from the drugs, but the room was dead silent. With the hood over her head, she could chance opening her eyes. A few dim rays filtered in through the dark material, and Matrix strained to make out the shadows of the walls. A pungent, metallic odor of rust and dried blood hung in the stale air. *Well, that's not very sanitary.* They really go all out here to sell the whole captive torture chamber setting. Although, not knowing how long she had been unconscious made it difficult to say for certain that she had not been moved.

With no sign of anything useful in the room, Matrix had no other choice than to let those holding her know she was awake. They would become tired of waiting for her soon enough, and she had gathered everything she could from her current position. So, making a show of waking up, she groaned and slowly lifted her head. Being awake for a while had allowed her mind to clear the drugs significantly, but she was selling the idea that she was still disoriented in hopes that they would let their guard down.

When Matrix sat up to signal she was awake, she was surprised that no one immediately came in to begin questioning her. But with no other options, she settled into the uncomfortable chair to wait for them to make their move.

It had been two hours and forty-seven minutes since she had been left supposedly alone in the room with no sign of anyone coming. Matrix scanned the room for the umpteenth time, checking to see if she had missed anything. Ever since she had awakened, she had not been able to shake the feeling that someone was watching her. The faintest sound from the edges of the room, a dark blur in the corner of her vision, but nothing concrete. The mind is a powerful thing, capable of playing tricks on you and making you sense things that are not there. It was entirely possible that she was beginning to jump at shadows. Her body was once again set on full alert as yet another shift in the room set her on edge. She sat completely rigid, holding her breath, and tracking the barely perceived object of her torment.

Gradually, the sounds became more noticeable. Footsteps would echo softly around her before fading into the silence. Whatever games they were playing with her were beginning to mess with her head. As a trained operative, not being able to see your enemy was a very uncomfortable feeling. It could mean the difference between life or death. It felt as though she were surrounded by threats, but she had no way of knowing what was there.

Another set of barely tangible footsteps echoed off to her right, and her head swiveled to track them. As they once again faded into the abyss surrounding her, a very solid fist, seemingly from nowhere, collided with the side of her head.

The other three Phoenixes had awakened that morning to the sound of a struggle coming from the cell on the far right. They each sat silently trying to determine what was happening. After the short-lived commotion died down, three men they easily recognized as guards carried Matrix's motionless form from her cell. Blade watched the scene take place, powerless to intervene.

Once the guards left with their package, the door locked behind them, leaving an uncomfortable silence in their wake.

It was likely they had taken her for questioning about Project Marionette. None of the others had any information, so it was unlikely they would be questioned about its function or location. If Matrix's theory was right and the Organization did intend the convert them, then any other information would be extracted from the team once they were under the Organization's control.

When conducting an interrogation, often the most infuriating thing for the interrogator is when their prisoner has taken a vow of silence. However, the man conducting the interrogation of the Phoenix team member Matrix Cross may like to refute that assumption.

"...And you should probably consider getting an electrician down here to check that wiring," Matrix suggested facetiously. Matrix had to bite back a fit of laughter at the look on her interrogator's face.

"Major Lockfire will be here soon. You better shut up if you want to still be here when he arrives," the frustrated man threatened, making sure he got his point across.

Matrix stopped talking, purposely flashing a scared look up at the man's threat. She had been rattling off some hilarious nonsense, if she did say so herself, about anything from the interior decorating of the room to the interrogator's hair nonstop since the man decided to show himself. In a rather rude way, Matrix mentally added.

The man crossed his arms, obviously proud of his work until Matrix dropped the act. She let out a short laugh shaking her head slowly and all traces of fear instantly faded from her face and a bright smile took its place. "Well, since you're offering and like I already said, it stinks in here, I wouldn't mind heading somewhere with more comfortable chairs," she said, batting her eyelashes at him and patting the arms of her chair.

The interrogator growled at Matrix's teasing. He would be happy when the Major got there, and he could get to work. He was going to enjoy breaking this one. Some may have qualms with hurting a child, but he did not get into this side of the business because of his outstanding compassion.

"Well, I guess it would be rude to leave without telling the Major," Matrix sighed, "That would be awkward."

No, he was definitely going to enjoy this.

When Major Lockfire arrived, his lead interrogator and the Phoenix girl were locked in a heated staring contest. Matrix smirked having noticed the Major enter but realizing her opponent had not. Major Lockfire loudly cleared his throat to alert the man that he had arrived. Matrix fought off another fit of laughter as the startled man jerked to attention. Upon learning that his superior had arrived. The interrogator gave Matrix one last fleeting glare before moving to stand beside the Major.

"Good Morning, Miss Cross. I hope you have been enjoying your stay," Major Lockfire greeted, his usual cheeky tone reinstated since their last encounter.

However, Matrix noticed that he had a slight air of apprehension about him and smiled to herself. Matrix inclined her head to the man. "Good morning, Major. Kicked any puppies today?" she asked, matching his tone.

Major Lockfire snorted in response, not offended by her words. "Well, I am glad to see you have a better sense of humor than your teammates appear to have," the Major said with a chuckle.

Matrix shrugged humming. "When I want to," she countered.

"Well then," the Major said clapping his hands together, "time to get down to business."

The Major's tone had darkened, and Matrix was mentally preparing herself for what was to come. A sick smile appeared on the interrogator's face, and he disappeared into the shadows created by the dim, overhead light to retrieve his tools. Matrix reasoned that they would not want to do any permanent damage since they wanted to use her and her team, but that did not mean there were not a lot of options still on the table.

When the man came back into the light with a needle glinting in his hand, Matrix knew this was going to be a long day.

The interrogator flicked the syringe filled with an unknown clear liquid once and moved toward Matrix's left arm. Matrix leaned back into the open air behind her, earning an annoyed look that would be more fitting for a disobedient dog. Matrix's eyes flicked apprehensively down at the needle and back up the man.

"No point in resisting," he murmured as he took her arm in his hand.

Matrix jerked biting at his hand as the cool metal slid under her skin, but the interrogator just laughed swatting away the minor annoyance as he gently injected the needle's contents into her veins.

"Settle down, you will only make it worse," the man mockingly soothed her.

As soon as he was finished and had released her arm, Matrix jerked back the offended appendage shooting him a defiant look through the hair in her face.

Major Lockfire smirked at the violated glare pinned on him. He would not be smirking if she hadn't been tied down, Matrix thought as a series of scenarios played out in her mind.

The Major gave her a long-suffering sigh, "Relax, that was just something to help you be a bit more cooperative."

"If you know as much about me as you say, then you should know you're not getting anything out of me," Matrix fired at the Major.

Major Lockfire clasped his hands behind his back as he began to circle around his bound captive. "Despite what you may believe, we are not the bad guys, Miss Cross," Major Lockfire implored, "You, on the other hand, I am not convinced."

Matrix stayed quiet. She was unimpressed by his words.

The Major continued the speech he had planned for the young operative since their last encounter. "You have spent the last ten years working under Dr. Jamison's control,

Matrix glared at the Major's word choice.

"Isn't that correct?" he pressed.

Matrix had none of her former respect left for that man.

If you asked her, that man got what he deserved. She chose to voice as much, "Jamison made us, but he betrayed our purpose. I have no regrets."

Their purpose? Major Lockfire considered that for a moment. He knew that Alpha team turned on the doctor, but it still was not clear why. Their file said that they had given their loyalty to both Dr. Jamison and their country. Could a part of her training have also influenced her turning on the trainer? Was this because he turned on the government?

"Let's start with something easy. What was your relationship with Dr. Ulrik Jamison?" the Major asked politely.

Matrix tilted her head narrowing her eyes at him. He smiled slightly at the action. The Phoenixes were not used to answering pointless questions, and he had already told her that he had their files. She knew he was just trying to get her talking.

"We know everything there is to know about Dr. Jamison, Miss Cross. There is no reason for you to resist," Major Lockfire stated, but received nothing but silence in return. That was fine, they were just beginning. "Alright then," he began after deciding to demonstrate a taste of his knowledge, "you were selected for his program at the age of four along with nineteen others. He both experimented on you and trained you to be his perfect weapons." The Major paused briefly to check that he had her full attention before continuing. He was not disappointed. "Yes, we have full psychological profiles for your entire team. You have a very impressive file, Miss Cross. Let's see, you were an excellent spy, somewhat of a chameleon I suppose you could say. Superior reflexes, eidetic memory, LLI, notes for expert marksmanship, linguistics, an IQ of 197..." he paused briefly at that, glancing up from the file to look at Matrix before closing, "just to list a few."

Matrix, however, gave little reaction beyond a slightly vacant stare. Apparently, her file neglected to add "part-time statue" to the girl's profile.

Suddenly, an idea came into Major Lockfire's mind. He recalled several notes made by Dr. Jamison that had caught his attention when reading through Matrix's training records. Despite the natural expression of the majority of emotional responses being mercilessly drilled out of the children, Cross's file had several notes about the girl still being very attuned to the emotions of others. Though she became very skilled at maintaining an impassive mask throughout her training, Dr. Jamison was concerned it could become a weakness as easily as an asset in the field. As an operative or a spy, not allowing any trace of the thoughts and emotions below the surface to be displayed was a vital component to ensuring you would make it out alive. There was no room for remorse for killing if that is what was asked of her.

"I also read that you are a bit of an empath," the Major said, "That must make the things you have to do more difficult."

Matrix had to resist the urge to smile at the Major's shift in approach. If he thought that he was going to get a reaction out of her by playing toward her emotions, then he did not pay enough attention to her file. That would be an amateur mistake.

"I was wondering though, what title do you prefer? Assassin, soldier, spy, agent, maybe special operative? You do so many jobs. It must be difficult, all those evils you have committed," he asked darkly.

He wasn't wrong. When she was first brought into the

program, she hated the things Dr. Jamison made her do. Her features tightened imperceptibly as memories floated through her mind in a dark haze. She lost innocence years ago, there was no going back.

"So, you know about his men in office," Matrix said abruptly.

Major Lockfire jumped at the suddenness of her words. He tilted his head at her trying to decipher their meaning. Realization took longer than it should have to gain a foothold, but when it did, he smiled. She was asking about the four government officials that Dr. Jamison had the Phoenixes abduct a few months back. That information would not have been in Dr. Jamison's official reports to his government liaison. She was testing him. Maybe she was deflecting as well, but he saw a hint of genuine curiosity in her previously vacant eyes. Again, he smiled at that. From what he understood, Dr. Jamison kept his team in the dark on anything outside of their objectives. He did not want them to become too independent and begin to form their own agendas. She must have pieced that information together for herself, but she was a genius, so he shouldn't have been surprised. In retrospect, that is probably why Dr. Jamison lost control of the Alpha team. He tried to stop them from asking questions and lost their trust, but he had taught them too well. They were smarter than him. Maybe when they were younger, he could get away with locking them in their rooms, but now they were not afraid of him. The Major had studied their files, and he knew them well. Dr. Jamison had put a lot of effort into conditioning his subjects to be absolutely compliant. It was one of his greatest fears that he could lose control, but he was blinded by arrogance. And, when the government wanted to shut him down because the risks were too great, that is when he turned on them and consequently contradicted the loyalties he had instilled in his team.

Major Lockfire was determined not to make the same mistakes. Dr. Jamison may have been a brilliant scientist, but he lacked the strength of a military man. The best approach to place himself as the authority figure was to assert his dominance over the Phoenixes. "We are a global organization, Miss Cross. It is our job to know," he said confidently.

The Major slowly maneuvered until he was leaning over Matrix menacingly with his hands on the arms of the chair she was cuffed in. "Don't worry, we have taken care of them," he murmured inches away from her face, his breath mixing with hers.

Matrix forced herself to resist leaning away from the uncomfortable presence. Showing her discomfort would only gratify him. He was still young and arrogant, overconfident in his skills. Eventually, the man pulled back, and Matrix allowed a bit of the tension to release from her body.

Major Lockfire turned his back to her and resumed pacing around the chair. She did not enjoy allowing someone to stand directly behind, so she did her best to subtly keep him in her line of sight.

"I believe we have wasted enough time, don't you? I say it's time we get down to business, shall we, Black Phoenix?" he announced enthusiastically.

Matrix's eyes snapped up to him in surprise at the use of her code name. "How..." she began to ask confused, but he interrupted her.

"The file," he supplied, "I was not bluffing. It's all in here. The doctor was a thorough man. He kept records of everything, and our men were able to make copies of it all.

Matrix shook her head minutely. The drugs they gave her must be kicking in, she should have known that.

"You say you ev'rything, then why d'you need me?" she asked, internally cringing at the slight slur in her words.

The major didn't immediately answer but instead continued to circle her like a shark waiting for the proper moment to strike.

Matrix continued to track his movements but instantly regretted turning her head quickly to catch him come around the other side. She felt her vision swimming as the room began to tilt on its axis. She batted her eyes rapidly in an unsuccessful attempt to blink away the unwelcome sensation and continued following the Major's movements.

"Don't fight it, it will only make things worse," the Major's voice sounded in front of her.

Wait, when had he gotten in front of her?

"We know you took it," he said, his voice sounding impossibly far away for the distance he was speaking from, "All you have to do is tell us where you hid the device."

Matrix shook her head violently like a toddler denying she stole a cookie. "Don't know what you're talkin' about," she giggled out, somehow both looking bitterly resolved and like she found the statement hilarious.

"You might as well tell us, considering you will be joining us soon enough," the Major said gently.

Matrix shook her head again, now appearing to be pouting but unable to cross her arms due to the restraints. "These are tight," she noted to no one in particular while looking down and wiggling her wrists in the cuffs.

"How much of that stuff did you give her?" the Major asked over his shoulder.

The interrogator smiled back, "Enough." Major Lockfire placed a hand under her chin and lifting her head to look into her eyes. "She's ready to begin," he called out, looking into her unfocused gaze pityingly.

Despite the drugs, Matrix was determined not to give him anything. He didn't know that she had seen all of the files on both her team and Project Marionette after breaking into Jamison's office, and that was one piece of information she intended to keep to herself.

CHAPTER 18

Liquid Life... or Death

When the interrogator first came forward with a needle, Matrix had begun preparing for a number of possibilities; truth serum, hallucinogens, the kind that set your skin on fire... Dr. Jamison had worked to build up an immunity to several drugs in their systems. Maybe she would get lucky. She had reminded herself that they couldn't kill her. They wanted her alive after this. But she also couldn't escape, she had no idea how to get back to the others. So, when the drugs began taking hold of her system, she placed her mind outside of her current situation. Blissfully detaching herself from the pain of the solid world.

"Wait, we can do this the easy way you know," Major Lockfire's words echoed in her head, "Like I said, we are not the bad guys."

Matrix had considered his offer for a moment. "The truth is... maybe you just weren't funny. That's why they don't like you," she had said softly, thinking back to their interaction when the Major first arrived. Or at least she hoped it had come out coherent enough through the drugs.

The Major had starred at her in confusion before realizing that she was talking about him. That was just before a cloth was forced over her face. "Have it your way," he sneered.

A part of her had wanted to believe him, believe that the Organization wasn't just another collection of corrupt military agents that wanted to exploit her abilities, but she wasn't that naïve.

The cloth was ripped from her face. Bright lights, they were too bright. Her eyes couldn't focus. It was like fire against her retinas, and she squeezed her eyes shut against blinding inferno. Why was it suddenly so bright? Everything was muffled and there was a sharp ringing pressing down on her skull. Was she still underwater? Shadows moved above her conversing with each other, but she was beyond comprehension. Daggers tore at her lungs from the inside. She was sure she was going to die this time.

Her body was jerked unkindly to the side and a strong force collided with her spine. "Was she not dying fast enough for them?" her mind screamed as another solid hit impacted her abused body. Another hit and her lungs contracted, expelling a volume of the intrusive liquid. She lay on her side over the side of the chair gasping as each spasm sent more of the icy liquid bubbling past her lips. Her body arched as her lungs tried to draw in more oxygen than was physically possible. Each gasping breath sent another cough ripping out of her throat in the opposite direction. It was an internal battle of two opposing forces fighting for control and for survival.

Major Lockfire watched as the girl lulled to the side struggling for each breath heaved past her nostrils. He walked up to her side and patted her back in an action that almost seemed comforting. "You can stop this," he whispered softly in her ear. "I can end this now," he emphasized, tenderly brushing her cheek, "It brings me no pleasure to cause you pain." "We know you have the device. All you have do is tell us where you hid it," he urged her for the hundredth time that day.

His patience was wearing thin. The drugs combined with hours of torture and waterboarding should have been enough to make a grown man spill his guts hours ago, much less a little girl.

He gently lifted her head, forcing her to look him in the eye. "Will you tell me the location of Project Marionette?" he asked one last time. Her eyes were slipping closed and he was afraid that was going to be his answer, but she surprised him yet again when she slowly but adamantly began to shake her head.

Major Lockfire dropped his chin and let out an exhausted sigh. "Very well," he said pushing himself to a standing position. "Again!" he demanded slapping his hands together and causing the girl to jerk slightly away from the sudden sound. Major Lockfire motioned to the interrogator to take his place and stepped back to observe. He would break the stubborn teen. No matter how long it took.

Matrix watched the beads of water chasing each other down the disordered strands of her hair to land in the small puddle forming on the floor beneath her.

She thought back to the small drain on the floor she had been eying apprehensively when they removed the hood. They were well below ground, there was only one reason she could think of that they would need a drain like that in an interrogation room. She had known the hours that followed would not be fun, and she was right.

With no one there to see her, Matrix pulled her knees in tighter as she replayed the day's events in her mind. She was soaking wet by the time they were finished with her, and the cold cement floor offered little warmth.

This was exactly what she was trained for. Hours of torture at the hands of Jamison, or training as he called it, ensured that she would not be giving the Major what he wanted. She knew how to deal with pain and psychological torment. What had broken sixteen other children is what made the remaining four strong.

Another droplet descended into the glistening pool shattering the illusion of reality. Fluid ripples radiated from the point of contact as though they were fleeing from the darkness that water represented. As though they could feel what it had done.

She saw the world for the darkness it contained. One look behind the veil and your soul is forever stained. People blanket themselves in ignorance, but no one in this world is safe and none are innocent.

CHAPTER 19

Mission First

On the third day, Matrix stiffly pushed herself off of the cold cell floor. They could be back for her any time now. Major Lockfire had not relented in his interrogation techniques. There was a surprising number of interrogation methods that left no visible scars. A myriad of drug combinations and psychological tortures, needles inserted under the fingernails, electricity (Oh, yes. She was familiar with that one.), but simple brute force seemed to be the Major's favorite yesterday.

Matrix gingerly lifted the hem of her torn, bloodied shirt. It was becoming impossible to tell where one bruise literally bled into another. An impressive feat by the Major, considering that she was not one to bruise easily. She only hoped that it would all be worth it. The team had devised their plan and were prepared to execute it after the night shift change. One benefit of being dragged back to her cell late at night was that she was able to take notice of the time and guards on duty.

The minutes began to bleed into hours, but still, no one came to take her for her daily fun with the Major. Matrix knew the others would likely be growing concerned as well, but there was nothing they could do but wait. The Organization was good. Without access to any of their tools, even Corbet couldn't get past the locks on their cells.

Matrix didn't sleep that night. Her mind raced through all of the possible reasons that they hadn't taken her that day. And there was one possibility that stood out above all others. They found the device. As many alternatives as her mind generated, she always came back to that one scenario. So, she lay on the cheap, lumpy excuse for a cot with her eyes wide open until morning. Morning, that was something she missed. Even though she could predict the time with reasonable accuracy, something about having nothing to indicate the hour was disconcerting. At least Jamison had allowed them a clock. These people were probably afraid they would build something to escape with if they gave them anything more technologically advanced than a blanket. And they were right. It would probably be an all-out race to see who could get out first.

The following days were stressful. Any time a guard would enter, the energy in the room would become tangible. Only to fade as they left after completing their task. Ivy was becoming restless. Matrix was afraid she would pull something drastic if an opportunity to put their plan into action did not present itself soon. Corbet had been doing his best to reel in his teammate. But if Matrix was honest with herself, she wasn't far behind Ivy. So, when after four days of silence, Major Lockfire appeared in front of her cell in person, Matrix was not going to miss her chance. Seven days in an Org. cell was long enough for her.

It was late in the evening, but Major Lockfire didn't want to wait to deliver the good news.

He confidently strode into the Phoenix's private cell block with a broad smile on his face. Three of the four Phoenixes lined up at the glass as he took the same position he had the first time he introduced himself to the elite team; front and center. His eyes sparkled as they passed over each of his prisoners, earning an indifferent look from Corbet, some screaming and pounding on the glass from Ivy, some annoyance from Matrix, and a steely glare from Blade. The Major lingered on Blade who was still eyeing him from his seat on his cot, before winking and moving to stand in front of Matrix.

"Miss Cross," he greeted, "It's been a while."

Her expression said everything he needed to know about how she felt about seeing him again. There was just something about the man that made her want to rip out his ego and stuff it down his throat.

"Not happy to see me?" he laughed. Silence. "I don't suppose you would like to tell me where you stashed the device now, would you?" he asked playfully.

The corner of Matrix's lips twitched up slightly before

she stepped up within inches from the Major, only an inch-thick barrier of glass dividing them. She leaned in ever so slightly closer, batting her eyes before politely offering a suggestion of where he could go.

"Rude, but that's alright," he said turning to move where they could all see him again.

He was holding something back, and Matrix had an uneasy feeling that she knew what it was.

"Oh, don't look as though I'm about to introduce you to your firing squad," the Major chastised. "I bring good news," he announced, a wicked smile settling on his face, "You will all be joining us today."

An unreadable mask quickly fell into place on Matrix's face, but inside she was berating herself. This is the moment she had been fearing. They found the device. The weight of the realization came crashing down on her like a plane, and years of practice were the only thing that allowed her to keep her reaction unreadable. Everything they had fought for was ripped from her in an instant. But it was not over yet, no chance she was going down that easily. They would have to take her kicking and screaming.

The tension in the room had amplified tenfold, but Major Lockfire didn't seem to mind. He floated across the room as though he hadn't a care in the world, even with four deadly teens glaring daggers into his soul.

"I must say, I would have expected better hide and seek skills from someone with your background," he said directed at Matrix.

The girl shrugged, that was a child's game, right? She eventually decided that was right, "We didn't play games in the Phoenix program."

The Major hummed lightly. "Maybe you should have," he retorted infuriatingly. "After all, I made a decent seeker," he laughed.

Matrix stared at him half confused and half annoyed.

"Fine," Major Lockfire deflated dramatically (He still believed he was funny.), "A maintenance crew found your little hiding spot in the SUV."

Matrix hoped that the others were not laughing at her sad attempt to keep the Organization from getting their hands on the device, but she knew that if the roles were reversed then she likely would.

"However, I must say that it didn't exactly match the specs reported by our men," he said with mock confusion, "In fact, the boys in the lab believe there were two important chips missing. The Major was holding up two fingers to emphasize the statistic.

Matrix smirked slightly deciding to play along. "I wonder how that could have happened," she said out loud, feigning shock.

Major Lockfire gave her a knowing look. "It's alright, it took some time, but our lab was able to get it functioning again," he said proudly, "Our scientists were able to fill in most of the blanks. We have a collection of the brightest minds in science in our employment." "In fact, I believe they even made some improvements of their own," he added, "Dr. Jamison may have been brilliant, but the fresh blood here has a slight edge over that old-timer."

Matrix's smile slipped at the Major's confident words.

"I suppose we should be thanking you for those upgrades," the smug man added after seeing her disappointment. He had no shame for toying with the girl. She had shaken him when they first met, and he resented her for managing to get past his defenses.

"I believe it would only be right if Miss Cross here had the honor of joining us first," Major Lockfire said smiling cruelly and motioning for the guards to take her.

This was her opportunity. Now or never. When the guard unlocked her cell, Matrix stormed the door. The advantage of not resisting when they took her before was now showing because the guards were not ready for the attack directed their way.

The first guard went down easily. A rib-cracking knee to the midsection followed by an elbow strike to the back of his head once he doubled over, sent the man crumbling to the floor. The other guard, right behind the first, moved forward to subdue the girl that had just taken down his friend but was greeted with a palm heel to the nose followed by several throat strikes. The guard struggled to restrain the girl, but one final, well-placed strike sent him to lie beside his comrade.

Major Lockfire stood back wide-eyed until the second guard fell. Then, the realization that he was next finally had the military men stepping into action, but Matrix had gained the upper hand before the Major could gain his footing. A side kick to the solar plexus sent the air fleeing from his lungs while a hard metal object, the butt of the first guard's gun, impacted his temple sending his world into darkness.

Matrix frantically hauled the Major's unconscious body close enough for his limp arm to reach the hand scanner and free her teammates. All three of her teammates were anxiously waiting at the door to their cells as Matrix dragged the Major down the cell block. As they were released, they gathered weapons from the downed guards. Once out, there was a shared silent communication. They each knew the plan. Matrix had shared all of the data she had gathered in her time outside of her cell. She was still the only one that had seen any part of the base other than the cells, but she had carefully cataloged each turn in her mind and shared every detail with her team. Soon the moment passed, and they were all hurrying out of their prison.

There were no guards immediately standing outside of the cell room, so they smoothly broke off into their respective teams. If they were separate, the odds of one team making it was increased. There was a staircase to the left side of the building that the guards led Matrix down when taking her to the interrogator, but she had also noticed a staircase to the right of the open space ground-level when she was first brought in. Assuming the building was semi-symmetrical it should not be difficult to locate the access to that stairwell. The next obstacle would be the electronic hand scanners that seemed to be located everywhere in the high-tech base. They couldn't drag Major Lockfire through the base with them, but as Corbet pointed out to Ivy, they wouldn't have time to saw through the bone with a pocketknife to take a hand with them either.

Corbet, as the hacker and technical genius of the group, had been studying the hand scanners in the cell and devised a theory of how to get past them.

Alpha team moved through the winding halls with Matrix in the lead. It was likely someone had reported their absence by now, so time was of the essence. Matrix had given Beta team the location of each camera on the way to the left staircase, but it was much harder to predict where one would be on their current path.

Matrix peered around the next corner with a small pocket mirror she lifted of a guard several days ago. It would be faster if they could take out the cameras as they went, but it would be just as easy to follow a trail of broken security cameras as it would their image on the feed.

Matrix evaluated the scene that appeared on the mirror in her hand while Blade kept watch over their surroundings. Once she determined the greatest blind spots, she indicated the path that would avoid detection based on the angle of the camera, and they did their best to stay out of sight. Matrix moved first and Blade trustingly followed her path. The pair continued that method of avoiding detection until they reached the staircase.

Once they reached the hand scanner, Matrix traded places with Blade. She was still slightly surprised that they had not run into any more Org. employees since they escaped their cells. She supposed that if they could avoid being detected, the first ones to notice their absence would be the scientists in the lab the guards had intended to take Matrix to as the first one to be converted by Project Marionette. It was impossible to know how many prisoners were currently being held, so the other three's empty cells could go unnoticed long enough to give them a fair head start.

Blade glanced over his shoulder at Matrix who had her gun raised and was scanning for threats. She had an intense look on her face, he recognized it as the expression she wore when she was deep in thought analyzing a situation. He trusted her to alert him if anyone was coming, so he devoted his attention to bypassing the lock. His hand felt in his pocket for the knife he had liberated from one of the unconscious guards and aimed it toward the panel. He frowned slightly at the noticeable tremor in his hand but took a deep steadying breath and began to pry off the outer portion of the scanner's casing.

Matrix was focused on watching their backs and didn't notice her partner's struggles. A faint click behind her signaled that the door was being opened. She offered Blade a ghost of a smile and ducked through the door he held open for her.

Again, as the one with the best idea of where they were going, Matrix took point. An arrangement that Blade was silently grateful for. Matrix nimbly began ascending the stairs, six levels according to her memory, but Blade had no doubt in her directions. Blade bit down on his lower lip, eying the stairs warily. He watched as she cleared the immediate area, before nodding for him to follow. After the first few steps, his vision grayed slightly, and he leaned against the rail with his eyes closed against the dizziness accompanying it. *Mission first*, he repeated in his mind. He sucked in a shaky breath and forced the air out, willing it to leave him somewhat steadier. Digging into his reserves, Blade pushed himself off the railing and did his best to stay a step behind Matrix. If Matrix noticed him falter, she didn't comment, and if she slowed her pace, he didn't call her on it.

The cameras in the staircase were everywhere. They would inevitably be caught regardless of how careful they were. So, stealth was sacrificed in favor of efficiency. They were three flights in when they heard shouts from above. The pair glanced at each other. There was no point in turning back. That would only solidify their defeat. Alpha team moved forward at a quickened pace in order to gain as much ground as possible. Boots could be heard pounding against the stairs from above, but they could only hope they were still valued alive.

Both of the Phoenixes moved silently in a way befitting of an assassin. It gave them an edge over their opponents. The loud stomping of boots on concrete stairs told them exactly how far away the men were, despite the echo of the staircase. When the men were almost upon them, they slowed their pace in anticipation. Despite being outnumbered, they silently prepared to ambush the security team once they were within striking distance. They anxiously waited until they were seconds away from being discovered; the only sound detectable was the slightly rapid breath of the Alpha team members. With their weapons raised, they rounded the final corner, firing shots into the unprepared men at the front of the pack.

The echo of the shots was deafening in the small space, but necessary to gain an early advantage. After dropping the front men, Matrix quickly engaged the second row. The men were still too densely packed to fire their weapons without risking hitting their own, and the men in front were too busily involved in the fight to use their rifles.

While Matrix dealt with the guards, Blade took advantage of the rest to catch his breath. However, he felt bad leaving his teammate to do all of the work. She could handle herself in a fight, but the conditions were not in her favor. Blade mentally readied himself for the fight and called out to his teammate.

Matrix instinctually counted eleven men in-between dodging and delivering strikes. *This was doable, right?* Her fist connected solidly with another man's jaw, and she used his momentum to send him over the railing to join two of his comrades already resting on the ground below.

"Matrix!" she heard Blade call out behind her. He was motioning her to send some of the security guards toward him. Matrix considered it for a moment. She knew something was wrong, that much was obvious, but she knew he wouldn't complain until the objective was complete. Mission first.

Blade watched as his partner considered what he was asking her to do. Obviously, he had not been as convincing as he had thought. He shifted uncomfortably under her examining gaze, but it didn't last long before she was forced to return her full attention to the fight. She seemed apprehensive but sidestepped an attacker and used his momentum to pass him behind her.

The progress went quicker with two fighting against the current, but Matrix was still reserving the majority of the security guards for herself. Blade forced himself not to be offended by what was obviously an attempt to spare him, but they were taught that the mission was all that mattered, and this felt like Matrix was purposely protecting him. He would not admit it, but it bruised his ego to have her protect him. But any insecurity was gone the moment the final guard was sent over the railing, and too soon, they were moving again.

They were one floor away from the exit on the ground floor when a shot impacted the wall inches from Matrix's head. The young operative flinched back, ducking for cover. "Crap," she muttered under her breath.

Blade tapped his partner on the shoulder, and she turned to see what was wrong. She was still concerned, but he seemed to do fine during the fight.

"You missed one," he teased, pointing in the general direction of the shooter.

Matrix laughed in spite of herself. She really hoped he was not deliriously right now. She didn't believe either of them would ever admit it out loud, but they had developed a close bond through their shared struggle to survive. But that didn't stop her from punching him in the shoulder for the snarky comment.

Matrix tossed an empty magazine out into the open to draw out the shooter. When the man took the bait, Matrix fired. "Are you happy now? It's clear," she asked waving her hand out for him to move, but she eventually took the lead again when he didn't immediately move. She had deduced her partner was injured before being brought base, but he wasn't very forthcoming with information and there was no time to stop and evaluate. If something was wrong, he would tell her. Mission first.

The team breached the ground level, only to meet more resistance. Blade was fading on her the last flight of stairs. But fortunately, now that they were out of the stairwell, the pair didn't hesitate to fire off as many shots as they needed to get the job done.

Once their path was cleared, Alpha team cautiously moved toward the nearest exit. It was late, but it appeared there were still a lot of Org. agents working on the ground floor. Agents that were now rushing in semi-restrained chaos. It still was not clear exactly what kind of base they had been brought to or exactly what kind of people were in their employment or even what kind of business they were involved in.

It was risky, but if they could make it out the front exit, Matrix had seen the positioning of the defenses and could keep them in the blind spots. The chaos as a result of the shots fired allowed them a small margin of error to go undetected. There were people running away from the shots and others toward where they were fired. The open layout of the ground floor made hiding more difficult, but slowly, they worked their way across the floor. They could hear people shouting from the area they had just evacuated, leaving a pile of injured security guards in their wake. Some were shouting for medical assistance, but others were shouting for those responsible to be found.

By the time they made it to the ground floor, there was no mistaking that someone had noticed that they were missing. It looked like the base was just beginning to go on lockdown. The team they took out in the stairwell must have been a group sent to check level six for a breach. It was impossible to tell exactly when they noticed that the Phoenixes were missing, but the shooter in the stairwell must have confirmed that prisoners were loose and initiated the lockdown.

Metal shields began descending from the ceiling at an alarming rate, to seal off all exits. If they didn't move now, it would all be over. The pair had taken cover behind a large, currently unmanned desk to the right of the main doors, but their position could be compromised at any second. With the base going into lockdown, there was no time for subtly.

With little warning, Matrix jerked Blade along beside her as she abandoned their cover. Blade took his cue from Matrix, and they raised their guns, shooting their way through the guard station. Guards and agents alike turned to fire on the elite team. Bullets were flying at them from every direction, but there was no time to address each threat when their window for escape was literally closing. It was a full sprint to the doors, and it was a miracle that neither of them was hit. Years of intense target practice allowed them to eliminate those with a clear shot before they were able to act first.

Once they reached the glass doors, Matrix fired several rounds into the glass without bothering to check if it was unlocked. With a forceful kick that sent glass shards flying from the impact, Alpha team finally was able to step into the cool night air. As Blade rushed through the door behind her, Matrix fluidly exchanged her spent magazine, turned, and fired several shots to deter anyone from pursuing.

Much to her surprise, it appeared that they were not being followed.

"Wonder why they let us go?" Blade asked in a gravelly voice.

Matrix was about to say that she didn't know when something caught her attention out of the corner of her eye. "They didn't. Move!" came the urgent response.

It took a while for Blade's sluggish mind to catch up, but by that time, Matrix had already grabbed his arm and began dragging him along.

Blade let out a choked cry at the sudden shift in momentum, as his feet did their best to comply with the order.

Matrix mentally reprimanded herself for not remembering the now very important bit of data earlier. On her way into the base, she spotted four large panels on the outside of the building. While they may have appeared innocent at the time and easily could have been mistaken as a design feature, the not-so-innocent panels had now sprouted machine guns that were raining lead projectiles down on the teenage special operatives.

The ground erupted inches behind their heels as they raced for cover.

Man, I hate being shot at. So, why does it happen so darn often? Blade whined internally.

"I think they are linked to the motion sensors on the cameras," Matrix yelled over the commotion, "We need to find a dead spot."

They were both out of breath, and her voice was shaking in time with her feet pounding the turf, making it harder to understand her over the sound of the eruption of deadly metal nuggets right behind him. And that was just too much for Blade's shaky cognitive abilities to grasp at the moment. However, what he could grasp right now was the idea of sleep. And, the more he thought about it, the better it sounded.

As if sensing her partner's wavering train of thought, Matrix decided that moment to grab his torso and tackle him to the ground. The automated fire that had been following them tilled the ground that they had just vacated before suddenly halting.

Matrix allowed herself a moment to simply breathe and reassure herself that she was still alive. That had been a lot closer than she was comfortable with, and it had only been an educated guess that the spot where they were currently lying would be hidden from the sensors. The cameras could only detect motion so far down next to the base due to a slight mobility weakness Matrix noticed in their mounting fixture. For the most part, the cameras were set up to be stationary, and figuring out where the cameras could not overlap was actually quite easy for someone with her abilities if given a bit of time.

Matrix turned to offer her partner a bit of privacy as he did his best to regain control over his rapid breathing. It wasn't much, but Blade was immensely grateful for the small act of consideration. While he did that, Matrix took the opportunity to reevaluate their options.

There were patrols moving along the fence watching for them and the guard stations she noticed on the way in had searchlights scanning the open ground. If the patrols were able to move freely near the fence and the automatic fire had ceased once Matrix tacked them almost against the side of the structure, then it was highly probable that their purpose was to prevent someone from crossing between the two. That was great news. It meant that they would be free to move, as long as they stayed against the base, but that still left roughly eighty of the ninety yards to the fence for them to cross without being shot.

"They are looking for us. We need to move," Matrix whispered, shaking her partner's shoulder.

The look she received for the action was nothing short of pouting. After becoming horizontal, becoming vertical was not making his to-do list anytime soon. In fact, Blade was not sure if getting up would still be listed under the abilities section in his file. He would have to speak to someone about that when he woke up.

Matrix watched as her partner's eyes begin to slide closed again. She wanted nothing more than to allow him to drift blissfully into oblivion, but if she allowed that now, it would be much less pleasant when he did reawaken. Matrix shook his shoulder again eliciting a low groan from the prone Phoenix. She had allowed him to handle himself and not pressed for a list of injuries, but now she was wondering if it had been a mistake to not press him for an answer. Neither of them were the most forthcoming in that department, but she respected him too much to press. Matrix winced in sympathy at what she was about to do. Matrix leaned forward and lifted his arm. She then located the pressure point a couple of inches up from his elbow and below the bicep and began to press firmly with her thumb. The pain would hopefully make him alert.

Instinctually, Blade's other hand shot out to grab and twist her wrist painfully. However, while still disagreeable, the action lacked its typical strength, so Matrix held the position and allowed him to fully awaken.

Slowly recognition sparked in his green eyes. Blade released her with a mumbled apology, but Matrix waved him off.

"We both deserved it," she said smirking.

"What did I do?" Blade slurred indignantly.

Now convinced that her partner wasn't passing out behind her, Matrix turned to address the next issue, but not without answering his question first. "You were supposed to stay awake," she said dryly, but the words held no malice.

Matrix turned her back to her partner and began picking out the motion sensors. There were five cameras visible from her current position. If her theory that the motion sensors linked to the cameras were also the ones being used to control the automated weapons, taking them out would disable the guns. Matrix checked her magazine which was already half empty. They were running dangerously low on ammunition. The spare magazines they grabbed off the guards in the stairwell were quickly being depleted, so she really hoped that her theory was right.

Matrix leveled her weapon with the sights in alignment over the first camera. Most marksmen would laugh at the sight of a fourteen-year-old girl with a handgun and iron sights lining up for a shot at this distance, but they would be surprised. Matrix adjusted for the rise and fall of the bullet across the distance and smoothly squeezed the trigger. She visualized the projectile hitting its mark, and reality reflected that result. The bullet satisfyingly shattered the lens and ripped through the wiring on the other side. She then turned, repeating the process for the other four cameras with lethal efficiency. Deadly accuracy was just one of her many gifts.

Blade watched his partner take out the cameras in quick succession from his position on the ground. He was usually the sniper on the team, but he couldn't help being impressed with his partner's proficiency. Not that he would admit it.

Matrix turned to see her partner staring up at her with, from what she could tell in the low lighting, was something close to a smile on his face. The side of her mouth quirked up a bit at seeing this side of her usually stoic teammate. "You will get your turn," she assured him as she painstakingly hoisted him to his feet.

Once upright, Matrix frowned as he leaned most of his weight into the side of the base. Awkwardly, she nudged him offering her shoulder to begin moving. He seemed to consider it a moment before shaking his head and starting forward on his own. *Good*, Matrix thought. It would have been much more concerning if he had accepted her offer.

Once the guards realized that Matrix had also disabled the automatic weapons when she took out the cameras, the enemy would also be free to chase them. Until then, Alpha team needed to put as much distance between them and the exit they escaped through as possible.

Despite taking out the cameras, the two stayed concealed in the shadows of the base. Neither of them were quite willing to test Matrix's theory without it being necessary. Staying in the shadows kept them hidden from the potentially functioning motion sensors as well as human eyes. The biggest chance of detection left was the guard towers. Their searchlights were still methodically sweeping the grounds, and Matrix had not forgotten the night vision capabilities she noticed on her way in. It was possible they believed the two were dead. That much gunfire followed by silence often indicated that outcome, but without bodies, they would continue searching. Staying ahead of their search would be key. Which brought up their next concern.

Their current pace could best be described as either slow hurrying or a fast turtle. Matrix was doing her best not to become frustrated with their current pace, but their training had not instilled patience for this type of scenario. In fact, she would already have been ordered to leave her teammate by now, had Jamison been giving the orders. A fact that she was sure would already have crossed Blade's mind. Particularly when she silently moved to help him.

"So," Matrix began hesitantly, "Are you going to tell me what happened?" Her voice was light with a hint of amusement and just a touch of annoyance. Openly showing concern wasn't really her style and bordered on dangerous in her line of work. So, the question was phrased more along the lines of "what did you do this time?" rather than "are you ok?"

By now, Blade was half walking and half being dragged along by his partner. Apparently conscious hadn't meant that his body would be cooperating. He had been running on adrenaline and stubbornness, but now those were beginning to bleed from his system as well. Speaking of which, Matrix's question had taken him by surprise. He had been practically expecting her to leave him. Honestly, he couldn't really say what he would do in her position. He knew that the guards would be coming for them soon, but neither of them had anything left but each other and the hazy idea of freedom.

Blade's eyes darted over to meet hers before they fell to his feet. Though the sixteen-year-old stood at just under 5'8 in comparison to Matrix at around 5'4, the awkward angle placed them almost eye to eye. Matrix could feel him stiffen against her at the question, so she patiently waited, not pressing him for an answer. The two continued to creep around the base with Matrix scanning the perimeter for a weak point in the fence.

Suddenly, Blade shoots a hand out to the wall for additional support as his knees buckle beneath his.

Surprised by the sudden additional weight, Matrix barely avoids falling on top of her already injured teammate.

"Ready to tell me what's wrong now?" she questions, simultaneously urging him up. She's leaning over him with a hand around his waist when he reaches out and places a hand on her arm. He knows she's not a tactile person, so the gesture grabs her attention. He's looking at her with nothing but pain and determination in his eyes, but it's not the determination she's looking for.

Against the odds, they had made it above ground. They could see freedom just on the other side of the fence. Matrix bit her lip to stop from saying anything she would regret. No, they are too close for this. She shakes head her at him knowing what's coming next. She could be stubborn too.

"Leave me," he says weakly.

Disregarding his words, Matrix drops beside her long-time teammate and friend and begins to scan for the source of the problem. It was a friendship that never should have happened, but she had already experienced what it was like to be on her own. They can see the searchlights closing in behind them.

"There's no time," Blade tries to tell her, but she vehemently ignores his protests.

It didn't take long before Matrix found the growing red stain Blade's black uniform had been hiding. "The fighting must have reopened the wound," she comments mostly to herself.

"Yeah, well..." whatever Blade was about to say was abruptly cut off by a strangled cry.

"Have to keep pressure on that or you'll bleed out," she says smirking. The exasperated look he gives her makes it worth it. They have a unique relationship, almost like a brother and sister. They can get away with fighting and causing each other pain and still not have the other take it personally. But this time the prodding didn't provide the same lighthearted break in tension it usually held. She could feel heat radiating from the area around where the wound was and winced sympathetically as a slight shift in pressure caused him to bite back a yelp of pain. This was not good.

"Leave me," he implores her one last time, a bit more forcefully, but the searchlight has already landed on them. Storm clouds gather in her eyes, but she doesn't care. The bright light glaring down on them creates a glow around the girl leaning over him. Her deep blue eyes are gazing into his, and he decides that if this was the last image he ever saw, it would not be the worst way he had imagined going. He is barely skirting the edge of consciousness when he hears her solemn words.

"Not this time."

The three words were brimming with unchecked emotion, but it didn't matter anymore. Matrix could hear them approaching behind her. "Not this time," she echoed softly.

"Hands in the air!" a gruff voice commanded behind her, and the tell-tale sound of several military rifles aiming at her back served to punctuate the words. Matrix numbly complied, slowly lifting her empty hands above her head. She heard the heavy steps approaching behind her but didn't flinch as her hands were roughly pulled behind her. Her eyes never strayed from her fallen teammate, even as she was pulled away.

CHAPTER 20

Your Mind Is My Mind

The calm, cool night belied the turmoil and chaos that hung around the walls of the Organization's base. Agents stood in their tracks as the two teens that had shot their way out only earlier that night, were dragged back into the clutch of armed security guards. It was hard to miss how young they were, a fact that many of the agents found more than a little disturbing. Now that they weren't pointing weapons at anyone, it was difficult to believe that the two vulnerable looking children being paraded through the shattered doors were the same ones who had just felled a small army of guards. The images just didn't line up.

As she was led back through the path of destruction left by their escape attempt, Matrix couldn't help but reminisce amidst the destruction they had caused. Hurricane Alpha did some serious damage.

Cleaning crews had already begun sweeping up the broken glass and debris from the firefight, but it would be a long time before the base was fully restored. Bullet holes from both sides littered the walls, and perhaps the glass features were not the best design choice for this line of work. The sheer amount of broken... everything would certainly be putting a dent in someone's funds. Not to mention the more expensive pieces of machinery outside.

The worst part of being marched back, however, was the countless pairs of eyes transfixed on her position as she was paraded to the end of her life. She could feel the eyes on her and could see into the souls of the ones she dared to meet. Burning hatred, confusion, fear, ice-cold malice, but it was the sympathy that caught her off guard. Anger she could meet with a steely gaze of indifference, but why would anyone here feel sympathetic toward her? Not that there was an overwhelming amount of that in the crowd that had gathered, but one would be baffling. Had they not seen what they had done to earn their play for freedom? Matrix couldn't bring herself to linger on those connections.

The question only served to raise more questions. The strongest in her mind being, *who were these people?* Never before had Matrix ever seen the people she dealt with display anything other than fear or a burning desire to extinguish her flame. At least not after they discovered who she was.

Two of the guards that brought her in shoved her down onto a medical chair, but it does not escape her notice that there are several more positioned around the lab and outside the door.

"Glad to see I made an impression," Matrix laughs dryly.

Slow, dramatic claps signal the arrival of Major Lockfire. "That you did, Miss Cross," he says as he walks in. "That was truly impressive," the Major began. "You know, I was beginning to believe that the 'legend of the Phoenixes,'" he sarcastically says in a goofy voice complete with finger quotes, "wasn't all it was cracked up to be." Matrix shrugs her shoulders choosing not to comment. "But you," he says shaking his finger at her, "you impressed me."

The expression the Major received after complimenting the girl was not what he had expected. Matrix gave the man in front of her a perplexed look, clearly trying to determine his intentions.

"Do you find something I said confusing?" he asked, his amused voice drawing out the words.

"We failed," she said simply, as though it should have been the most obvious explanation in the world.

"Ah," Major Lockfire said nodding his head. "Well, yes," he said rubbing the bruise forming above his cheekbone, "but you left an impression."

Matrix smiled mischievously at her handy work while the Major continued. "That was the farthest anyone has ever made it from level six," the Major informed her with what sounded like genuine respect. But the words he said next sent shivers down the young operative's spine. "You are going to make an excellent asset."

After that statement, the Major stepped back and the medical staff wasted no time moving forward to connect various wires and monitors to her body. As the mass of men and women converged around her, the reality that there was no escape this time was quickly sinking in, and Matrix had to fight to keep the panic out of her eyes.

She was no stranger to scientists hooking her up to one kind of machine or another, but that did not make what was happening any less unsettling. The lab tech that came to attach a set of electrodes to her temple offered a timid smile, but the dangerous look that flashed across Matrix's eyes caused the young tech to pale slightly before completing the task and quickly running off.

While the lab staff went about their business, Major Lockfire stood close by watching on with twisted satisfaction. "Don't look as though you are about to be executed," he told her sarcastically, "We are offering you a new life."

Matrix realized that in his own twisted way, Major Lockfire might actually believe in the altruistic reasoning he was giving her for the use of Project Marionette to convert her and her team, but that did not change her opinion of what they were doing to her.

"At the cost of my own," she volleyed back with a biting intensity that didn't quite match her young appearance.

"Don't be so dramatic," the Major patronized. "These lovely people tell me they have made some significant improvements to your Dr. Jamison's crude design," he said gesturing widely around the room.

The raised eyebrow told the Major just how much Matrix trusted those in the room, including him.

Deciding that the less delicate approach was more likely to achieve results, Major Lockfire gave her the straightforward version. "That shell of a human being you saw in the sublevel of Dr. Jamison's base would not be any more useful to us than handing a monkey a live grenade. That is not what we have in store for you," he assured her, "You are a precision tool, not a chainsaw."

It was not much, but Matrix did find some comfort in his words. Even if she was slightly surprised that he knew the details of her involvement in Dr. Jamison's lab. There was no way she would trust him, but she did trust the logic his words contained. And it was nice to hear that she was not going to be turned into a brainless body that would strike at anything in its path. That's always a bonus.

"Will she remember anything I tell her now?" Major Lockfire leaned over and asked one of the scientists in the room.

The scientist, barely looking up from her work, answered with a coy smile, "Only if you want her to." "Very good," the major nodded as the scientist's full attention returned to her work.

Matrix watched the conversation between Major Lockfire and the scientist with concealed curiosity. Even though he kept his voice low, Matrix could still make out what the Major was saying. When he began turning to face her again, Matrix quickly averted her eyes.

"Miss Cross," Major Lockfire called to gain the attention of the young operative who was now glaring down the tech attempting to insert an IV into her left arm, "While our scientists are getting ready, I would like to brief you on the nature of the organization you will be joining shortly."

That got Matrix's attention. Her head quickly snapped toward the Major, not bothering to hide her interest anymore. Major Lockfire laughed lightly at the reaction but didn't keep the girl waiting.

While scientists continued to prepare her, Matrix

listened as Major Lockfire gave her the condensed version of the story.

"Outside of this base, the Organization does not exist. Our reach is global, we have people in every government and every regime. The Organization helps maintain order in the world, but we are neither inherently good nor evil. Our job is to do what is necessary, but the higher-ups can be swayed by the right person, if you know what I mean. Our ranks consist of the best of the best," the Major says, making a show of straitening his uniform, "We have assimilated men and women from all over the world, both for military and strategic operations. Generally, an agent is assigned work in their native country and often never leaves their previous job. It is only a special few that work as true Organization operatives. These untethered operatives are known as Vortex agents. They work independently of foreign governments or private establishments and typically have a specific skillset or our highest clearance. Our ranks are based on multiple factors; skill, clearance level, and how far one is willing to go to maintain world order. We understand that some have... moral impediments, and we take that into consideration when giving assignments. I am sure you are wondering where you are going to fit into all this," the Major said, flashing a knowing smile at Matrix before continuing. "You are going to be one of our Vortex agents. Named for their power and intensity, lightning efficiency, and the fact that trying to hold down any information on one is like trying to pin down the wind in a tornado," Major Lockfire finished with a chuckle.

Matrix raised an eyebrow at the Major's eccentric choice of words.

"Our tech guys are pretty good at covering our teams' tracks. They are practically invisible," he elaborated.

Matrix knew someone like that. Thinking of her team's hacker caused Matrix to suddenly realize that she didn't know if Corbet and Ivy had managed to escape, but before she or Major Lockfire could say anymore, one of the scientists announced that they were ready.

Matrix saw the familiar blue light emanating from the sphere as Project Marionette was brought to life. A few of the scientists began to explain what was going to happen, and she actually appreciated the gesture, even if she still despised them for what they are doing to her. It was possible that they were not all the enemy, but that wouldn't stop her from doing anything necessary if it meant escaping. Apparently, the Organization's scientists developed a way to use Marionette to target specific parts of the brain and implant or block certain memories without damaging the patient's mind. It sounded more precise than what she had seen in the files from Jamison's office, but still not far from the original idea.

Matrix had witnessed what happened when the process was not properly completed, and she genuinely hoped these scientists knew what they were doing. If she had to choose, she would rather end up as a loyal agent of the Organization than a mindless stimulus-response being.

CHAPTER 21

Reborn Again

Matrix did not regret anything that had happened. Not turning on Dr. Jamison, not destroying the base she had spent most of her life in, not even getting into that SUV, and certainly not staying with her partner. Regret is a pointless waste of time, energy, and sanity. The past is set. There is no point wishing you had done something differently. Learn from your mistakes and move forward into the future with a clear sense of direction.

Blade would be fine. They still wanted him, so they would keep him alive. Dr. Jamison would say her greatest weakness was that she cared. Maybe he was right. But she had made it out from under his control, and she was not going down again that easily. This is not going to be the end. She already tried leaving everything behind once. That was not the answer. She cared, maybe that was her weakness, but next time, she would get everyone out. That was her real mission. Not just an objective to be completed no matter the cost. Yes, it is a weakness. Oh well... screw you, Dr. Jamison. That was her last thought as everything she was began to slip away. It didn't hurt, so she allowed herself to fall into the oblivion.

"She is going under. We can begin the reconditioning now," one of the scientists announced.

The lab gradually picked up pace as scientists began moving about with various tools and equipment. Major Lockfire was ushered out to watch the procedure from behind a glass viewing window.

"How long will it take?" he asked the tech who had escorted him to the viewing room.

"Several hours at least," the tech answered casually turning the rejoin the lab.

Major Lockfire reached out and placed a hand on his arm to stop the tech from leaving. "Why so long?" he asked, shocked by the answer he had received.

"We are messing around in her brain to make a new person with a device that was basically just finished being created this morning. Everything has to be perfect, or you are not going to like the results. The human mind wasn't designed to be tampered with," the tech answered sounding slightly more annoyed as he went. Having to explain the complexity of the delicate procedure they were about to perform to a military man who blows things up for a living was not included in his job description.

Major Lockfire nodded, oblivious to the tech's inner

ranting, and the tech left to return to his job.

Eighteen hours and forty-two minutes. That was how long the scientists spent working on the newest member of the Organization.

Major Lockfire woke up around noon the next morning and headed to the cafeteria in search of food. It had been late when the procedure to convert Phoenix team member Matrix Cross began, but it was considered too much of a risk to hold her any longer than necessary after her near escape.

Major Lockfire grabbed a large cup of coffee and a tray of mediocre cafeteria food and headed for a vacant table. Once seated, the first thing he did was take a large swig of his coffee. He had left sometime during the third hour of the procedure with the intention of sleeping until noon. "Mission accomplished," he mumbled raising his mug and taking another swig of the dark liquid.

The Major had left multiple guards in his place to ensure the safety of the scientists working in the lab. They may have sedated that girl, but he had seen her file and would not put it past her to take them all out in her sleep. They had orders to contact him when the girl was awake, but until then he had his own responsibilities to handle. Top of the list; coffee.

Major Lockfire went about as normal and was just finishing up his work for the day when he received the call. The Major was down to the lab in a matter of minutes to see for himself if the procedure had been a success.

"How is our femme fatale doing?" Major Lockfire asked falling into step with the scientist that met him. The scientist looked over to the Major smiling as he pushed open the door to reveal the girl in question. "She's perfect."

Flash forward five years:

"Good morning, agent Cross," Colonel Lockfire greeted, approaching one of his best operatives.

"Good morning, Sir," Matrix Cross responded in a pleasant, formal tone.

"I have an assignment for you…" the Colonel said raising a file.

A smile formed across the operative's face as she took the file from his outstretched hand. "When do I leave?"

ABOUT THE AUTHOR

Raven Gray is a strong young woman who believes all girls and young women can be powerful and brilliant. She enjoys competition and has accumulated many championships as a martial artist and competitive gymnast. Her loves are human psychology, quantum physics, and the four greyhounds who share her home in the foothills of North Carolina.